SELKIE

MORTAR AND PESTLE SERIES

BOOK 1

SYDNEY WINWARD

A PART OF

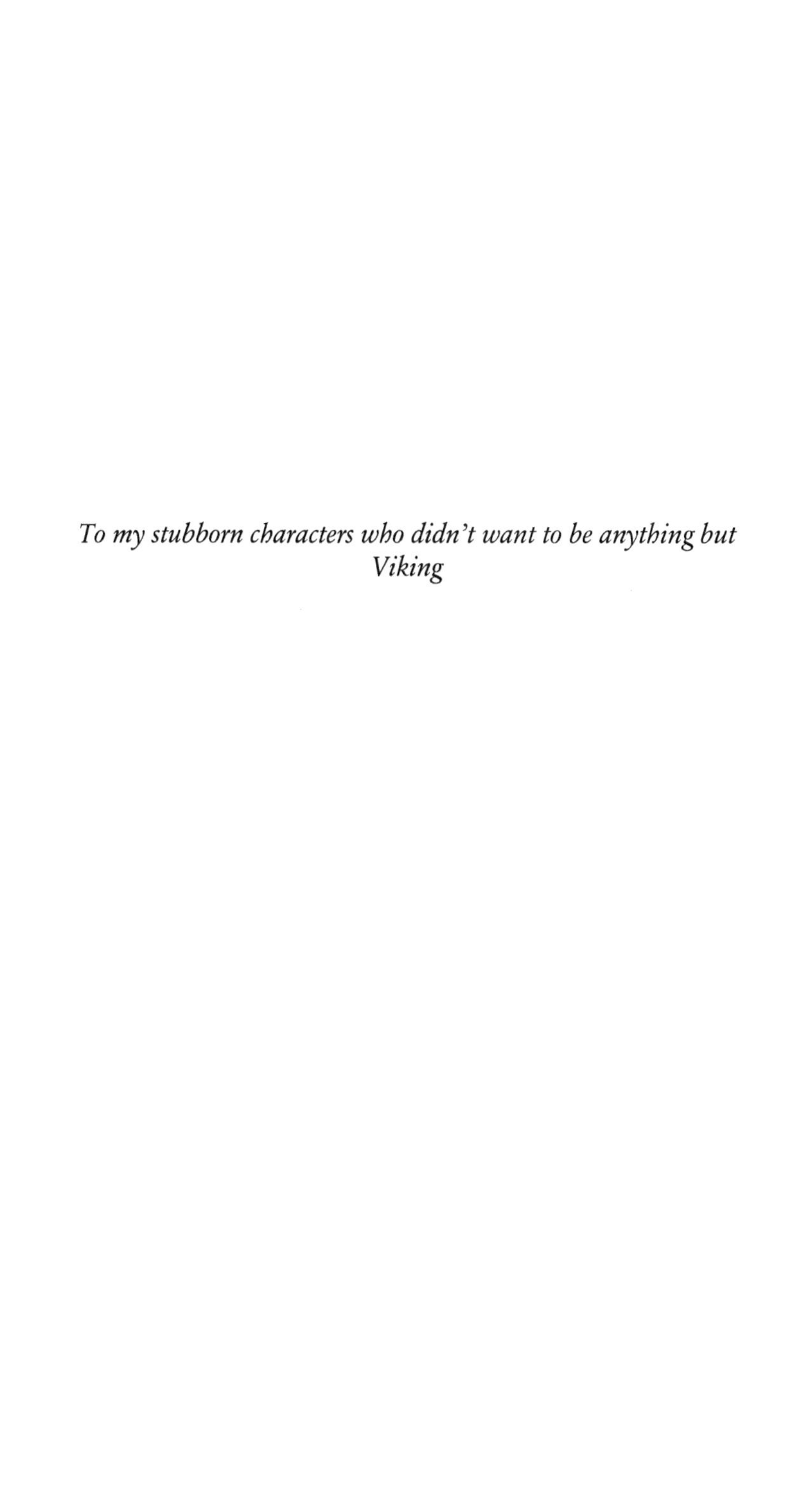

To my stubborn characters who didn't want to be anything but Viking

A wisp of smoke, a swirl of promise, a breath of destiny…a message within the Mortar & Pestle for those who want to believe.

Throughout time people have sought their heart's desire. But true love is often elusive.

Carved with ancient Norse runes, the Mortar & Pestle shows paths to happily-ever-afters.

Once you capture the Mortar & Pestle's scent of magic, you'll want to read all seven individual romances.

 *Selkie*

How can he marry one woman when his heart sings for another?

 *Seeker*

Nock, draw, release. If her arrow hits its mark, will it prevent war...and secure her destined soulmate?

 *Quartermaster*

Can the love of a pirate heal the wounds inflicted by a gentleman?

 *Sea Hunter*

On the turbulent high seas, an archeologist must protect a historic shipwreck from treasure hunters—not fall for one.

 *Revamped*

An energy vampire hungry for love meets the wisecracking woman of his parents' nightmares.

 *Trickster*

Can she heal the trickster before he breaks her heart?

 *Artist*

Stuck at a retreat with her ex, Lexi is torn between reviving her art and rekindling an old romance.

CHAPTER 1

Denmark, 900 A.D.

K laus Lovik spat out a mouthful of dirt and coughed when the dust-filled air settled in his lungs. He covered his mouth and nose in the crook of his elbow and peered into the gloom.

Darkness.

The faintest streaks of light entered the tomb between the cracks of piled rocks, illuminating the particles in the air. But otherwise, he could barely see his hands, let alone the space before him.

He scooted forward on his hands and knees, holding in a cough when the top of his head loosened the dirt from the mound of rock above him. The grave slanted farther until barely enough space remained between the shallow roof and the floor. Dirt wriggled beneath his fingernails as he clawed forward, intent on entering the confines of death to prove himself worthy.

Of his heritage.

Of his bride.

Dirt rained over his head, momentarily blinding him. He held his breath, his heart beating wildly within his chest. He prayed to Odin that he wouldn't be buried alive in the same grave his father had been buried in after he'd died.

After a moment, the air settled once more, and he wasted no time as he clawed the rest of the way to the cavern just large enough for him to sit. Another ray of light broke through cracks in the rocks.

His heart caught.

His father's ship rested within the small space. Covered. Unopened. Waiting.

Each breath he took became harder the longer he stayed in the burial mound, and his lungs screamed for deliverance. Steeling his emotions, he wiped his filthy hands on his already dirty breeches and slowly opened the wooden cover.

Barely visible in the darkness, his father lay in the peacefulness of death with broken weapons and other significant items from his life scattered around him. A jarl circlet rested upon his sunken brow, his skin now leathery with decay instead of full of life and vigor. In his cold, still hands lay the family sword, which his brother, Anders, had placed there earlier for the ceremony before the wedding. The metal gave off a beautiful sheen despite the scars embedded in the metal from many battles won.

And a few lost...

Klaus pressed a kiss to the blue gem in the center of the circlet, and despite his lungs now starting to seize from lack of air, he prayed for guidance through his journey and for the gods to lend him aid and protection.

Finally, he pried the sword from his deceased father's grip, replaced the lid, and clambered back out of the tomb, hardly sparing a thought for anything but the desperate need to resurface for air.

Dirt clung to his clothing, his hair, and his face as he got closer…closer…closer…

At last, he gasped the moment his head broke the surface of the grave. He triumphantly raised the sword, which was followed by a chorus of "Huzza!"

Anders grabbed onto his hand and hauled him to his feet. A couple dozen kinsmen ruffed up his hair, squeezed his shoulder, and cheered for his victory. Despite wanting to fall to the grassy earth as he recovered from the endeavor, he instead lifted the sword above his head. A thunderous cheer filled the gravesite, followed by a rumble of thunder across the cloudy sky.

A good omen.

"Thor cries his approval for you today, Brodir," Anders said, clapping him on the shoulder. A year younger than him, Anders was almost a spitting image of himself with light brown hair, eyes as blue as the sea, and a similar strong build. His brother was only slightly shorter and preferred fishing to hunting. Klaus, on the other hand, had the patience of a rolling storm and the stubborn heart of a bull. When he hunted, he would bring home dinner or not return at all.

When a second wave of thunder moved overhead, Klaus glanced toward the sea stretching from one side of their homeland to the other in a crescent-moon shape. A dense fog crept steadily toward the rocky shore, nearing the village with every passing moment, putting him ill at ease. It made it more difficult for the watchmen to spot the dangers lurking in the waters such as enemy Norsemen, witches, or…

A shudder ran down his spine.

Or selkies.

His attention moved from the section of beach littered with large, rough boulders to the battered and empty boat still ashore. Cursed, everyone called it, as the vessel had once held a dying man with a tale almost too incredible for belief. A tale of how his entire island was drowned by a single selkie only days ago.

"Klaus," a female voice said moments before someone touched his arm. He jumped, startled out of his reverie to find his mother chuckling at him. "Where are you today?"

"Not here, it would seem. He's too busy envisioning the marital bed." Anders laughed, and Klaus whacked his brother in the shoulder.

"If you want to keep your ears," he growled, "then I suggest you shut your mouth."

"How many times have I heard that threat? You have yet to follow through."

When Klaus lunged forward to punch him again, Anders laughed and ducked out of reach. Instead, his mother took him by the elbow and licked her thumb. "You'd better get cleaned up. And fast." She smiled tightly, and despite his protests, she wiped dirt from his face with her spittle. "Your bride is waiting."

He took a deep breath and straightened his spine. With sword in hand, he had entered into death as a boy, and reemerged as a man reborn. Today, he was ready to take his bride.

As if intent on never letting him out of their sight, a few of the men—including his future father-in-law and brothers-in-law—accompanied him to the bath house where he cleaned the dirt from his skin and hair and dressed himself in his finest clothing. He tucked an ax into his belt for good luck and finally faced the men who had accompanied him.

His brother stepped forward, draped an ax-shaped necklace over his head, and placed a circlet over his brow, one with a stone as clear as glass sitting over his forehead. Though younger than him, his brother blessing him as chieftain on his wedding day symbolized his ancestors blessing him from their place in Valhalla.

Anders finished by kissing the stone and stepping back. Between the men in the room, they created a pathway to the door. A door that led to a new future.

Nerves tumbled in his stomach, but he refused to let it show. He strode outside, through the village consisting of longhouses, playing children, and plentiful gardens, and toward a grove of trees overlooking a vast blue ocean. Several dozen family members and friends—and a few enemies—waited on either side of him, surrounding an arch decorated with antlers, bones, and flowers with the backdrop of dark clouds, frenzied winds, and a crashing ocean.

And standing directly beneath the arch...

His bride awaited.

Lise wore a gown of red, her blonde hair adorned with a silver crown, smooth stones, and animal bones filed to a sharp point. She was tall enough for the top of her head to reach his chin. She was sturdy with wide birthing hips and an ample bosom to give him strong, healthy offspring. Beautiful. Perfect for childbearing. And an advantageous political match. Not only did she have a hefty dowry, but the blood feud between their villages would finally be settled. For good.

He clenched his fists and tried to maintain controlled, even breathing. His blood boiled at the mere sight of her, now and forever serving as a constant reminder of each one of his losses.

He eyed her family, now missing three brothers. His was missing one brother and a father.

No other option remained but to end the feud between their families. No more blood would be spilled after this day.

"I have been waiting all morning," Lise said quietly, running her hands over his chest to smooth his clothing. Of course, the action did not go unnoticed, and several jeers and lewd comments followed. A few insults as well. He ignored them. Not everyone was happy about their union, but he knew it would bring much-needed relief from ceaseless bloodshed.

Despite his own feelings on the matter.

"Aren't men supposed to do the waiting?" he replied just as quietly, barely restraining his teasing grin as he fought for mirth instead of disdain. "What with the numerous washing rituals for women?"

"I pity the lass who has to put up with your wit for the rest of her days." She straightened the silver hammer necklace, so it lay flat against his chest. "It's a good thing you have one thing going for you."

Her gaze roamed over him suggestively. He raised an amused eyebrow. He hardly knew this woman, but she possessed an admirable steel in her spirit.

Before they uttered another word to one another, his brother stepped forward, acting as *gothi* in his stead. Their audience quieted when Anders began the ceremony by summoning the ritual goat to the arch. In a quick flash of a blade, he sacrificed the animal and filled a wooden bowl with its blood. Beside him, Lise didn't even flinch. The steel in her eyes remained.

Klaus clasped Lise's hands, ignoring the nerves turning his stomach. Disquiet rumbled through his head. Spinning and swaying and pounding its fists against his skull. Something didn't feel right. His gut instinct had never been wrong. But what had him feeling like he stood on the edge of a cliff, bracing himself against an unforgiving tempest?

Surreptitiously, he glanced at the guests surrounding them. Distrust lingered in some expressions. But no outright malice.

He shifted his weight between his feet in an attempt to stave off his unfounded worry. The marriage contract weighed heavily on his mind. If they weren't married by today at sundown on Frigga's day, the contract was void, and the blood feud could resume in earnest. But they were so close to solidifying the contract.

Anders dipped a fir twig into the goat's blood and sprinkled it over their heads. Next, he used his fingers to smear blood from Klaus's forehead, down his nose, over his lips, and to the bottom of his chin, doing the same to Lise next.

The unease in Klaus's gut intensified as he pulled his family's sword free from its scabbard and exchanged it for the one Lise offered him. Next, they traded rings—his a thick band of silver with etchings of Odin's horns and hers a smaller band etched with intricate knots.

"Klaus," Lise hissed when Anders turned his back to retrieve the rope of binding. "You are turning green."

"I am not." Yet his queasy stomach betrayed him. Surely, his unease stemmed from missing almost half of his family for the ceremony. His older brother should have been there. His father should have been presiding over the wedding. Klaus shouldn't have been named chieftain. At least not yet. He felt too young for the role, even at seven and twenty.

Scratchy rope brushed his skin as Anders tied their clasped hands together. Lightning flashed across the sky, followed by quaking thunder. He jumped, startling them both when their hands were tied securely together and unable to break free.

He chuckled at himself, trying to hide the underlying nervousness stuck in his throat.

After a brief pause, Anders instructed to repeat after him. Klaus said, "I vow before Thor, Freyja, and Freyr—"

Thunk! Whiz! Snap!

Klaus hissed at unexpected pain as an arrow shot through the rope binding their hands and scratched the surface of his skin. The rope snapped and coiled at his feet. Time seemed to slow when a tendril of his own blood trailed down his wrist and plopped onto the ground, joining the sprinkling of rain overhead.

And then time snapped back to normal like a whip cracking through the air. Klaus's first instinct was to step in front of Lise and unsheath his ax.

His heart momentarily ceased beating.

A half dozen archers surrounded them, five of them pointing their weapons toward the guests, and one of them training an arrow on his heart. Who were they? Where had they come from?

Many of his kinsmen drew a weapon. But so did the enemy, more seeming to step out of thick, unnatural fog originating from the ocean waters.

Klaus eyed the fog crawling across the ground, his heart now beating wildly as he glanced from archer to archer and back to the fog. In the midst of the white haze, two pairs of feet appeared, followed by trousers and gray skirts. Finally, the faces belonging to the two apparitions appeared. The old hag's wiry ashen hair hung in her face, cracked lips turned into a snarl. An emerald witch pendant hung from her neck. And beside the witch...

Chieftain Oswald from an enemy clan.

The bleeding devil...

A scar ran from the corner of his eye to his cheek, a wicked triumph in the set of his mouth barely visible beneath his braided beard. He kept his sword sheathed as if convinced he had no need of it, though he held a bow in one hand, the arrow long since fired.

Oswald's smirk grew wider as his gaze darted toward the rope lying on the ground, and then to the blood smeared across Klaus's skin. "I was aiming for the bindings. But it seems I missed."

"What do you want?" Klaus gently pushed Lise farther behind him and hid her within the flowering foliage and bones of the arch. "You are interrupting our wedding."

"And just in time, too."

The man stepped forward, and Klaus's kinsmen did the same. However, the enemy archers were enough to keep anyone from attacking. Two well-aimed arrows were enough to fell both him and his brother. Who would be chieftain in their stead?

"Leave," Klaus ordered, turning his ax in a full circle to draw their attention to it. He would not let them come viking without a fight. Especially not today. "Or you will not leave this land alive."

A cackle of amusement escaped the witch followed by a chuckle from Oswald. "Are you so certain about that, Lovik?" He stepped close enough for Klaus to press his ax against the side of the man's neck. Disturbingly, Oswald didn't flinch. Rather, his eyebrows lifted in amusement. "I came for the *laskura*." He nodded to where Lise peeked her head around the arch. "She is to be my own bride."

Fury boiled his blood and drove him into the first attack. He swung his ax at Oswald, but at the last moment, the man deflected the blow with his sword.

"I challenge you to *holmgang*." Klaus spat in the man's face.

Nearby, his mother released a strangled sob, but nothing more.

Unease shifted through the crowd. Oswald's smirk fell into something that resembled anger. On his honor, Oswald would most likely face the issued challenge rather than flee and deem himself a coward.

Oswald shoved him away with his sword to his ax. "Seven days. You come to me. And come alone." The man eyed Lise. "But I will take her."

"May iron eat me before—" Mid-swing of his weapon, a bright green light flashed through the meadow, momentarily blinding him, followed by a fierce gust of wind. The blast knocked him backward into the arch, taking the entire structure down with him. His back slammed into a pile of bones cushioned by unforgiving flowers. The thorns pierced his skin like a hundred bee stings. His head spun against the blow. And when he opened his eyes, black dots as disorienting as a flock of ravens swarmed his vision.

"Klaus!" Lise screamed.

He scrambled to his feet and released a war cry as he lifted his weapon once more, fighting for balance as if the world beneath him tilted one way and then the other. But when his vision finally cleared, and the darkness dissipated…

Lise was gone.

And so was the enemy.

"No!" he shouted, kicking a pile of bones with the tip of his boot.

He helped his mother to her feet as everyone else also picked themselves up after the startling blow. Oswald's witch was powerful. Klaus wouldn't stand a chance in the *holmgang*, honor or no honor. But if he did nothing, he would lose his bride and his family's promise of safety.

His head spun as he glanced from his mother to Lise's father and finally to Anders. He could hardly think straight when fury burned hot beneath his skin. "Brodir," he called, approaching in only a few strides. "Are we married?" A legal marriage would help protect Lise from Oswald and his clan from her father's clan.

Anders grimaced and clutched his own hammer necklace in his palm. "You should be worrying about your upcoming challenge rather than your bride."

Klaus paced back and forth. Back and forth. "But are we married?"

"Uh…you…she…"

"Well, are we?" He stopped pacing and stood in front of his brother, arms crossed. Anders flinched away from his glare. These turn of events weren't Anders's fault. But the heat of a battle soon to be forged spread across his entire being.

Lowering his head, he replied, "No. You have not made vows with Thor, Freyja, and Freyr as witnesses. And then there is the matter of consummation…"

A frustrated cry climbed his throat and escaped like a bolt of Thor's lightning. He struck out at the bowl of goat blood, splattering the red liquid across the stones at his feet. Flecks dotted the toes of his boots and the bones of the arch Lise had hidden behind only minutes prior.

Without the wedding happening today, the marriage contract was void, and he was no longer promised. He had to fix this. But how?

Lise's father grabbed him roughly by the shirt. "If you don't get her back and renew this contract, it will be your head on the pike," he growled, bumping his chest against Klaus's in warning. "And next? His." The man motioned toward Anders pulling the arch into an upright position with several others helping beside him.

Klaus clenched his fist, staring coldly at the man responsible for his father's death. His father's honor dictated he should kill the man to avenge him. But he had his mother, brother, and two younger sisters to think about. Without this marriage, they could possibly lose more than just their honor. No matter how much it pained him, he had to make this right.

His gaze drifted toward the sea, now visible after the witch's unnatural fog had dispersed. The waves crashed against the rough shoreline in sync with the winds battling thunderstorms in the sky. One of the waves washed over the decaying, abandoned boat sitting on the rocky beach, sparking an idea. A dangerous yet foolproof idea.

He knew how to make this right—by giving Oswald an offer he couldn't possibly refuse.

CHAPTER 2

The chill of early morning shivered through the air. A hush settled upon the ocean, dawn taking its time in making an entrance. Creatures still slept, giving an appearance of absolute stillness.

Creatures and…

Humans.

Mayla Brior's head broke the surface of the icy water, her seal tail propelling her slowly toward the rugged shore, and her water magic helping her glide silently through the sea. She continuously scanned the land, searching for threats such as carnivorous animals.

And humans.

Several ships were docked on the shore, waiting for the next viking expedition or fishing excursion. Despite not feeling overly cold in the water, she shivered at the thought of running into one of those barbarians.

"*Mayla,*" her younger sister, Aislee, panted in their selkie language. "*I can no longer carry her. You need to take a turn.*"

She dove beneath the water and positioned herself beneath her eldest sister Erianna's flipper, taking her limp weight and swimming the rest of the way to land. The waves guided them until their flippers scraped against rough stones. Mayla breathed hard at the exertion, closing her eyes as small waves washed over them, retreated, and washed over them again. Cold. Salty. But filled with premature mourning.

They had traveled far from the destruction Erianna had wrought upon the distant village, desperate to escape the humans' hunting spears and fishing nets. Frantic to evade the danger.

After catching her breath, Mayla scanned the beach again. But aside from the boats, no one lingered on the shore. They had to change forms quickly before the world decided to wake.

Selkie magic stole across her being as she started the change. Her flippers thrashed. Her tail shuddered. And then her skin split from her chin to her stomach to her tail. The effort of shedding her seal skin stole what remained of her energy, and she lay naked on the beach in her human form next to her seal skin, her long brown hair drying in a wavy pattern as the minutes passed.

Exhaustion sat heavy on her chest. Sleep lay in wait should she give into the gentle lull and close her eyes for a few moments.

But she shakily forced herself onto her hands and knees, her human limbs weak with disuse. Her muscles trembled with the effort to stand, and when she only managed to lose her balance and fall back onto her hands and knees, she stopped trying.

"Erianna," she croaked, using her human voice for the first time in nearly a year. She shook her sister's shoulder, now in her human form as well. Like her, lovely brown spots covered her skin, marking her as a selkie. She was particularly fond of the three spots on her own cheek that matched the shade of her brown eyes.

When her sister simply groaned, she shook her shoulder again. "Erianna, you must forsake your seal form." Mayla stroked her elder sister's hair. "Otherwise, you will die."

Her sister's expression contorted in pain as she arched her back and breathed rapidly. In and out. In and out. "Never," she said through gritted teeth. "If I can't have my child and my seal form, then I would rather die."

Emotion burned her eyes, and she barely managed to blink back tears. Erianna had mated with a human, and when she returned to seek a life with him and their newborn babe, he'd taken the child and banished her back to the sea. Erianna had drowned the entire village to try to get her son back. Only to discover the child had passed in her lover's care.

"You must hear reason," she murmured, taking either side of her face. "You used too much magic destroying the village, and your selkie form is withering because of it. You *must* forsake it. Please. Live. For us."

"I cannot."

Aislee shifted away and sobbed, the sound escaping choked and strangled.

Mayla turned to find Erianna's seal pelt already starting to wither and dry. It was too late. Even if she *did* forsake it, she would still die.

A wail climbed her throat as she rested her forehead over her sister's heart. It beat slowly, also failing along with her pelt.

"I can heal you." Mayla placed her hands on her sister's shoulders, but Erianna weakly batted them away.

Her older sister shook her head. "Don't. It will take too much magic. And you have no vessel enough to contain it. I won't have you risking your life for me."

"But you are my family."

Erianna opened her mouth, but no sound escaped. Instead, she lifted her hand and brushed her fingers against the spots on Mayla's cheek. The faintest smile lifted the corners of her sister's lips before one final breath left her lungs, and her hand fell limp to her side.

Mayla stared down at her sister in shock, eyes wide and mouth falling open in disbelief. Erianna's chest no longer lifted with each breath. Her heart no longer beat within her chest. And her half-lidded eyes were glassy, the life gone from her body.

With trembling hands, she closed her sister's eyes the remainder of the way while Aislee's cries shook the very earth around them. The sky overhead darkened with grief. Waves crashed ferociously upon the shore. The water levels rose higher and higher, threatening to pull Erianna's body back into the depths of the sea.

But she deserved far more than a watery grave.

Numbness crawled across Mayla's body as she stood on shaky legs and dragged her older sister toward a grassy knoll. She fell twice, each time scraping her knees against unforgiving rocks. But finally, she laid Erianna on the grass, her expression peaceful in death.

Aislee wept next to her, but otherwise took one of Erianna's hands while Mayla took the other. Magic moved down their arms, into Erianna, and seeped into the ground beneath her body. Vines sprouted from the earth, flowering as they crawled across Erianna and covered her entirely. The vines pulled her body into the earth until she disappeared beneath. The only indication of her presence were the blooms sprouting from the grass in a mournful array of white blossoms.

Her stupor still reigned as she reached for a rock to use as a grave marker but froze when she felt something cold touch her neck.

Cold and sharp.

"Look what I found," a male voice said in the human tongue. Giddy. Triumphant. "Is this yours, by chance?"

Mayla spun around, hissing when the blade of a sword nicked her neck. Horror squeezed her chest when she found herself face to face with a human man.

And he held her pelt in his arms.

In a burst of speed, she harnessed her magic, and water shot out from the ocean and sprayed the man in the face. He gasped and sputtered as he stumbled backward, but he didn't drop her pelt. She sprayed him again, not allowing him to take another breath. He dropped to his knees.

The pelt remained in his arms.

Fine, then I will drown you on land.

A furrow marked her brow with the next stream of water. He made a choking sound and dropped onto his hands and knees, and when he tried to escape his certain death, she sprayed him harder and with more force.

He collapsed onto his stomach.

She rose to her feet, wobbling as she took a step forward and then another. She glanced around them only to find the rest of the beach abandoned, no other humans within sight.

In her momentary distraction, the man fought against the jet of water and lifted his sword. Her heart jumped to her throat when he held the weapon to the neck of her seal skin. A threat. A promise.

If she continued her attack, he would harm her skin and prevent her from returning to the sea.

All at once, she released her hold on her magic. Sea water splashed across the ground, and the man gasped in a desperate gulp of air. Wet brown hair stuck to his forehead. His soaked clothing clung to his body. And he continued to hack and cough up the water in his lungs.

"Go," she ordered Aislee in their selkie tongue, never taking her gaze off the sword far too close to her pelt for comfort. "I'll be right behind you."

"But—" she started to protest.

"I said *go*."

Behind her, she heard her younger sister scramble across the rocks, return to her skin, and dive into the water.

Mayla's chin trembled. She hadn't lost one sister today but two. She'd heard stories of men stealing a selkie's skin to wed them and bed them against their will lest harm come to their seal half.

She never thought it would happen to her.

How could she have been so careless?

The man finally stopped sputtering and climbed to his feet, swaying one way and then the other. His face was flushed red from all the coughing, his eyes bloodshot from exposure to the salty ocean.

He glanced behind her and frowned as if disappointed he'd only managed to catch one selkie instead of two. But then his attention returned to her. His gaze dipped downward to the lower half of her naked body but then shot back up to her eyes, a furious blush staining his cheeks.

"What do you want?" Mayla growled. The human language felt awkward on her tongue as if stumbling out of her throat and landing in a heap at her feet. There had been few instances in her life when she'd had to speak it.

"You will do exactly what I say, when I say it. Understand?" He spoke with an accent, and it took a moment to piece together his words. When she managed the feat, heat spiked her blood.

"Never."

He moved the sword closer to her seal skin, and she stepped forward to save it but stopped short when he shot her a warning glower.

"I do not believe you are in a position to say *no*."

"You are a monster."

The man raised an eyebrow, which disappeared into the wet hair still clinging to his forehead. "I'm not the one who drowned an entire civilization."

Mayla glanced toward her older sister's grave, the pain of grief consuming her once again. "I didn't do that." But she certainly knew who had.

As if to regain her attention, he motioned with his weapon toward a cluster of trees. "Move."

She stood still. "I will not marry you."

"I never said I wanted your hand."

She blinked back surprise but quickly schooled her expression as she guessed what he *did* want from her. Being a concubine was worse than being stuck in a forced marriage. But if she could steal back her skin before he noticed…

She lifted her head high and stumbled forward on wobbly legs, moving past him. But she inhaled sharply when he draped a damp cloak over her shoulders. She threw it off immediately, tossing it into a heap on the ground.

"I don't want your human clothing."

He picked it up and tried again. "You can't just wander around unclothed."

This time, she allowed him to drape the salty, damp cloak over her shoulders and hugged it tight around herself. Her hair reached her lower waist, drying in beautiful waves that covered her breasts. But she supposed it did not cover much else like the way humans covered their bodies from head to toe.

She tripped on the hem of the cloak but quickly righted herself, pulling her shoulders back, refusing to allow him to knock down her pride. As he followed closely behind, she eyed her skin. For him to lay his filthy hands on it caused her blood to simmer.

"I'll make a trade," she bartered. However, with her eyes on him rather than the path, she stumbled and might have fallen to her knees if he hadn't caught her by the elbow. She shoved him away. "I will give you anything your heart desires. Just return my skin and we may yet part ways amicably."

His eye twitched at her suggestion. "You tried to drown me. How is that amicable?"

"You touched my skin with your grimy barbarian hands."

"Barbarian? So says the woman who drowns unsuspecting men without so much as a greeting."

The hem of the cloak tangled in her legs, and this time he didn't move to catch her fast enough before she fell hard onto her hands and knees. Exhaustion rippled through her body, rendering her breathless. The muscles in her legs and back ached, along with the heartache festering in her chest. All she wanted to do was weep. For her sisters. For herself. For what misery her future might hold.

"Get up," the man ordered.

She shook her head, blinking back tears. She braced herself for another threat or perhaps even for him to strike her. No harm came upon her, and she dared to glance up to find him watching her cautiously yet with a softness in his eyes she had not witnessed in other barbarian men.

The softness disappeared so quickly that she questioned if she'd seen it in the first place.

"Daylight is fast approaching," he said, turning her attention to the skies lightening more with each breath. "I assure you I'm not the most dangerous *barbarian* you have fear of coming across. If you don't make haste, I will throw you over my shoulder."

Her fingers curled into fists. She thought she'd hated Erianna's lover. But now she realized it was only a flicker of a flame compared to what she was feeling for this man.

She eyed his shoulders. Even covered in a gray tunic, she could tell he was muscular beneath. His sleeves were rolled up to his elbows, exposing the impressive muscles in his forearms, too. She knew he could easily manage the feat of tossing her over his shoulder and reducing her pride to ashes.

"Have you no shame?" she shot back to give her more time to rest. "Is this how you treat your women here?"

His mouth twitched, showing the faintest hint of mirth. "I would be throwing another woman over my arm as I cross the threshold to our home, so I suppose so, ja."

Using her magic, she commanded one of the overhanging tree branches to smack him in the back of the shoulder. He yelped and spun around, glaring into the semi-darkness. "Try that again, selkie, and I will deliver the first cut to your skin."

She met his glare with one of her own. "It was a spider. I did nothing."

He raised an eyebrow. "It must have been a very large spider then. Quite the nuisance." He stooped and grabbed her elbow, hoisting her to her feet.

For the second time, she shoved him away and stumbled forward on agonized feet. Unused to walking on rough land for longer than a few minutes, they were beginning to blister. Whenever she slipped out of her seal skin, she usually kept a part of herself within the sea or within the comfort of warm sand. Never had she ventured so far inland.

Appalled by the idea of being carried like some animal, she fought through the pain and fatigue as he led her through the maze of trees until finally, the foliage broke to reveal sprawling farmland with large, domed buildings dotting the landscape. A beautiful green hue covered the land and a few rooftops. Sheep, cattle, and strange, round pink creatures grazed lazily in the early morning, creating an unexpected sense of peace. The initial surprise of finding beautiful scenery stole her breath away.

"What is that animal?" she asked, pointing to a creature with a rounded stomach like a cattle, a long brown neck, thin legs, and pointed ears.

He looked at her questioningly. "You mean a horse?"

"A horse," she murmured, forgetting herself and her situation. "Do you eat it?"

He shrugged. "Sometimes. Mostly, they're for riding and helping with farm work." But then his expression turned serious. "Hurry. People are beginning to wake."

The man gave her no time to protest as he took her elbow and steered her toward one of the large, domed buildings. They stole across green earth, ducked beneath a wooden fence, and then he looked around them before pulling her into a smaller building that smelled of dust, mildew, and dung.

Several more of the creatures called horses stood within confined stalls, and one even housed a brown and white milking cow. It lowed at her as they passed, its attention following her. She swore she could see sympathy in its large eyes as if it sensed what she was deep in her soul.

The stall at the end of the stable appeared to be empty, but when he pulled her inside, she inhaled sharply to realize it was occupied by another man lying on a bale of hay. The space beside him was indented slightly as if someone had been lying next to him recently.

Her captor swore under his breath and threw the hood of her cloak over her head just before the man on the hay bolted into an upright position.

"Klaus!" he said groggily, eyes bleary as he glanced around before his unfocused gaze settled on her. Each man looked remarkably similar with brown hair and brown eyes, making her wonder if they were related. "What hour is it?"

"Dawn," he answered. "Anders, you should be inside the longhouse."

The man named Anders glanced back and forth between them. "A bit early for a tryst, don't you think? I'm surprised you would risk it, what with your current situation—"

"This is *not* a tryst," Klaus seethed, but then Anders's mouth fell open as he peered closer at her, and then at her seal skin in Klaus's arms. She turned her face away, but she was sure he noticed the spots on her cheek anyway.

"That's a selkie!" Anders hissed, eyes wide. "What are you doing with her?"

"What does it look like? I'm trading her to Oswald. Lise for the selkie."

Anders shook his head, glanced toward the exit of the barn, and lowered his voice. "How did you catch one? Oh, never mind. You are a fool if you won't take the selkie for yourself. Just think about the rewards, Brodir. Other clans will fear us. They will *submit* to us! We will be untouchable. You can be more than just a chief. You can be a *king*."

"This is not just about Lise. By taking my bride from under my nose, Oswald has insulted my pride, my honor, and my family. But *I* captured the selkie and *I* will be the one to give her to him."

The younger man paced the floor, running a hand over his chin. "Then by all means, toss her back into the sea. It is better that no one has her rather than for Oswald to keep her under his wing."

Mayla's voice trembled the moment her words passed through her lips. "I have a name."

They both paused and turned to her as if forgetting she was there. The one called Klaus spoke. "Your name is of no concern to us."

She stood taller, straighter, and stared into his eyes. "I am Mayla Brior. You will refer to me by my name or not at all."

After a pregnant pause, Anders laughed, and Klaus scowled. The brother punched him in the shoulder. "Forget the sea," he wheezed. "Give her to me. I'll take your selkie as a bride *and* I'll prove myself worthy of the title of chieftain in your stead."

"She's not *my* selkie," Klaus huffed. "She will be Oswald's bride by the end of the week. In the meantime, *no one* is to know she's here. Not until I leave with her."

He turned away. She lunged for her seal skin in his arms, but he reacted quickly and held it just out of reach. The smooth pelt brushed her fingers but that was all she managed. Tears of frustration blurred her vision.

"I will hide this somewhere you can't find it. If you do everything I say, I will consider giving it back. Step out of line...and I will burn it."

She stepped closer to him until only a hand's width remained between them. The top of her head reached his shoulder, as he was a good deal taller than her. Her glare burned into him, and she hoped it thoroughly scalded him. "I'm sure being Oswald's bride would be far better than being yours."

Anders hooted with laughter while Klaus's ears flushed red.

But she wasn't done yet. "Lise must be happy to be rid of you."

"That's. Enough."

They glared at each other until it felt like fire crackled around them, creating imaginary smoke that climbed into her throat and snuffed the air out of her lungs. He broke eye contact first and stepped away.

"I will return with a dress for you to wear." He glanced down at her bare feet. "And shoes. And don't talk to anyone. Especially not Anders."

The moment Klaus disappeared from the barn, silence reigned in his stead. The cow broke the crisp morning atmosphere with a low, followed by a snort from a horse. Beside her, Anders studied her as if working out a puzzle in his mind. Uncomfortable with his scrutiny, she collapsed onto the bale of hay he'd previously occupied and rubbed her aching feet.

Anders didn't stay silent for long. "How did Klaus earn the title of chieftain, you ask?"

"I didn't ask."

He continued anyway in the same thick accent as his brother. "My brodir saved hundreds of lives with his cunning and weaponry skills when an enemy clan attacked years ago. He ended up saving our fadir, who had been the chief before him. Only to lose him months later to an ongoing blood feud." He reached for a sheathed sword leaning against the barn wall and inspected it in the dim light. "Naturally, Klaus was the best and most popular option for the next chieftain."

She couldn't imagine Klaus winning a popularity vote. The thought inspired a frown. "Why are you speaking to me?"

"Because *you* are amusing. I've never seen anyone get under Klaus's skin so easily." A grin spread across his face as he tied the sword onto his belt. "If things don't work out with Oswald or Klaus, I just might steal your pelt next."

"You insult me," she spat. "My skin is not an object to be passed around."

"Then Klaus better come to his senses soon and woo you." He grinned. "Or I will."

A chuckle escaped him as he, too, left the barn. Despite her protesting feet, she rushed to the exit and peered out. But Klaus was nowhere in sight. If he was hiding her skin, she had no idea where to start looking.

Moisture collected in her eyes and fell down her cheeks. She found herself trapped in a hopeless situation. And she didn't know how to escape.

CHAPTER 3

"Selkie," Klaus murmured from where he stood at the open door to the empty stall. He glanced anxiously toward the barn entrance and then back at the figure lying on the hay, covered in the cloak and face hiding beneath it. Several people had already come and gone, and he didn't want anyone to discover her there.

The woman didn't reply. Rather, the cloak rose up and down with each breath she took.

"Psst!" he tried again. "Selkie, wake up."

No answer.

He sighed and rolled his eyes. "Mayla, I brought you a dress."

She turned her head, and instead of finding a glare in her eyes like he'd expected, she regarded him cautiously. "I don't know how to wear a dress."

Heat scalded the back of his neck at the thought of helping her into it. The burn worsened when he worried over someone walking in and catching him doing it, coming to the wrong conclusion.

"Have you never worn clothing before?"

Surprisingly, she shook her head while scratching her arm where the hay must have poked her. "There is no need for it. I rarely interact with humans."

"Yet, you know our language."

"I know several. I learn them by watching and listening. I do spend a good deal of time on the shore in my seal form. I don't spend all of it in the sea."

The sound of two men walking past the barn and conversing spiked his pulse into a frenzy. He shut the stall door and held out the bundle of fabric in his arms, lowering his voice. "Come on, then. Let's make quick work of this."

Caution continued to live in her eyes as she slowly pushed herself into a sitting position, eyeing him, then the clothing, and him again. "I do not wish to look like a barbarian woman."

Klaus inhaled deeply, holding back a sharp retort as the woman tried his patience. Two days had passed since Oswald had taken his bride. Only five remained.

"Might I remind you—"

"Save your breath," she replied with a note of exhaustion in her voice. "You have made your point time and again. Show me how to wear this garment."

She stood and dropped his cloak from her shoulders. The heat of surprise shot from the floor and climbed his body. He averted his gaze to the bundle in his arms, putting intense focus into setting aside the leather shoes and unfolding the sark. He instructed her to raise her arms while he pulled it over her head but found it impossible to ignore the sparse brown spots on her skin from the side of her face to her bare shoulders. Some ranged in size from his fingernail to the size of his palm. The patterns were beautiful, like nothing he'd ever seen.

Taking a deep breath, he helped her into a light blue apron that went over the sark, attaching at the shoulders and draping down to her feet. His mother was a tall woman, so the hem almost brushed the floor. Unfortunately, she would likely trip again.

Finally, he finished with brooches at the shoulders and a leather belt around her waist. He turned her to face him, and his breath caught.

Her long, brown tresses dripped down her back and over her shoulders, showing off a beautiful face. Long brown lashes framed eyes the color of summer tree bark and rich earth. Lips as pink as a rose in bloom parted beneath his gaze.

"I'm not marrying you," she said suddenly, shoving him out of his confusing thoughts.

"I wasn't…" He huffed and pinched the bridge of his nose. Arguing would get them nowhere. The stubborn selkie was set in her ways, and he in his. "Stay hidden in here. We will depart at sundown. If you start to lose your mind with boredom, talk to the animals. I'm sure the lot of you have plenty in common."

A scowl formed on her face moments before she lashed out at him with her foot. However, she lost her balance and fell onto her backside. Even from her place on the ground, her glare remained.

"You certainly have a penchant for falling." He reached for her hand and pulled her to her feet but paused when his stomach became a knotted mess at the touch, at her nearness. A few brown selkie spots dotted her wrist and another one lay on the back of her hand, barely hidden beneath the edge of one of his fingers.

"Ah," he mumbled, quickly dropping her hand and backing away. "Tonight. I'll be back tonight." But as he turned around, he smacked into the door he'd forgotten he'd closed.

Heat burned his ears, and in a speedy movement, he slipped out of the stall and closed it behind him. The faster he traded her to Oswald the better. The selkie was beginning to mess with his head.

Klaus sharpened his ax with intense focus from where he sat on an outdoor stool beside the longhouse. He ran the weapon over the whetstone in smooth strokes, the repetitive movement keeping his fury at bay.

But just barely.

His pride was wounded. Out of all the things to happen on his wedding day, getting his bride snatched right before they were to exchange vows had been one of the worst outcomes.

For a moment, he allowed himself to agonize over the situation. Was Lise hurt? Afraid? Alone? If the pig snot took liberties with his future wife, he would cleave the man's head from his shoulders with this very ax. Even then, he would make sure Oswald and his witch never bothered them again with the selkie at his side.

At the thought of Mayla, he lifted his head to study the barn across the green field. Several servants and family members had entered and exited the structure, but no one had stormed out with a selkie in tow.

One of the reasons for his secrecy of the creature was to prevent any spies from getting back to Oswald before he managed to confront the man himself. Somehow, Oswald had known where and when to show up to the wedding. And why he wanted Lise of all women for his bride remained a mystery. Yes, the woman was beautiful and strong and resilient. But why her?

"May I sit with you?"

His mother approached, hands clasped in front of her and head bowed. Although she had been a slave many years ago, what she endured obviously still haunted her. She was not like many of the other women in the village. Rather, she was quiet, often unsure of herself, and jumped at loud noises.

The thought of his mother helpless at the end of Sten Borgen's blade flared his nostrils. This union was for her, and he would see it through to the end if it meant keeping her safe.

With a clenched jaw, he nodded to the space beside him on the log. She lowered herself next to him, a swish of a green sark brushing against him. Silence fell between them, charged with tension that only seemed to grow with each stroke of the whetstone.

"You are so much like your fadir," she started, and he winced but kept his attention on the repetitive movements of sharpening his blade. "Once he set his mind on something, there was little anyone could do to change his course of action."

"Fadir was a magnificent warrior." His brows furrowed as the memories of his death once again haunted his mind. Blood. Screams. Mourning. Loss.

"He also never knew when to lay down his weapon."

Klaus set the whetstone aside and rested his elbows on his knees, turning his head to give his mother his full attention. "To lay down my weapon is to subject my family to great suffering. I will forever stand between my family and the threat."

Her expression softened as she reached for him and began absently braiding small strands of his hair. He released a huff but otherwise allowed her to fuss in her own motherly way.

"The selkie you are hiding in the barn is a lovely young lady. I think you should release her."

He froze before snapping his attention to her, wincing when the action tugged on his scalp. "Did Anders tell you? I will wring his neck." He moved to stand but his mother pushed him back down and resumed braiding.

"He tells me everything." Her gentle hand rested on his shoulder. "Mayla is frightened. Just because she is not human like us does not mean you can treat her as I have been treated."

His stomach twisted, and he swallowed the lump in his throat. Slowly, his gaze lifted until it rested on the barn. His shoulders slumped, his weapon becoming slack in his hand. "I have not laid a hand on her."

"Because you are a good man." She rested her hand on his cheek and turned his head toward her. "But Oswald is not."

Rubbing his fingers over his temples, he closed his eyes and released a deep breath. "I cannot do as you ask without risking the safety of our family. I do not believe Oswald's threats are idle. If I hand over the selkie, we can finally know peace."

"But at what cost?"

"No matter what I do, there will be a heavy price to pay."

As silence filled the space between them, Klaus watched a flock of birds glide above them on gentle skies. Leaving the shore would not be difficult tonight, a small blessing in a world of uncertainty.

Finally, she squeezed his arm and stood. "Promise me. If you find another way, you must take it."

After a moment's hesitation, he nodded. "I give you my vow."

She fondly patted his cheek, and he watched her retreating back as she ventured toward the longhouse. Her words tarried far longer than her presence. He needed to hand the selkie over. For his family. For Lise. For his pride. What other choice could possibly remain?

A bag full of provisions for the journey lay at his feet, filled with dried fish, bread, cheese, and a water skin. Coupled with his ax, knife, and bow and arrows, he was ready to face the Norse chieftain.

Orange, yellow, and pink streaked across the sky, signaling the coming dusk. He blew out a long breath to steel his courage and stood. It was time.

Making sure no one looked his way, he slipped back into the barn as quietly as possible when he knew it was empty. He found the selkie taking several steps in the opposite direction before kicking her leg in agitation, only to do it again with the opposite leg. An amused grin found its way to his mouth. She clearly didn't like the shoes he'd given her to wear.

She jumped when she saw him, but then her expression relaxed. "Are these shoes supposed to feel so awful? I don't like wearing a covering over my feet."

Although he would never admit it out loud, he enjoyed listening to the woman's accent. It was light and airy and completely foreign. He couldn't place its origin.

He gestured to the hay, and when she sat, he knelt in front of her. He barely held back a snort of amusement. The laces were a mass of knots and loose ends. "You are going to trip over yourself, *sæta*. Allow me to help."

His fingers froze on one of the shoes, momentarily shocked at how easily the term of endearment had escaped his mouth. She stilled beneath his touch, as if she caught what he'd said. He didn't dare lift his gaze to witness her reaction. Rather, he focused on untangling the laces and slipping her shoes off…

…and he inhaled sharply.

Blisters covered the bottoms of her feet from her heels to her toes, the skin angry and red. "By Thor's hammer! We only walked from the ocean to the barn!" he cried but winced at the volume of his voice. He lowered it and met her gaze. "Have you never walked on land?"

It was clear she had not developed the necessary calluses to walk barefoot without injury.

"I have," she defended, head held high and hostility in her eyes. "But not far and not for long."

He ran a hand over his chin at the new conundrum. "I refuse to carry you this entire trip."

"Was it not you who threatened to throw me over your shoulder?"

Not able to help himself, he laughed. Her quick wit amused him.

A smile continued to linger on his face as he spotted the unused stockings he'd brought in earlier and slipped them on her feet to help protect her from further blistering, followed by her shoes. After, he tied the laces. A part of him felt silly for dressing a woman like he would a child, but it couldn't be helped. They were now pressed for time.

"Anders has agreed to retrieve you and hide you in my boat before my departure," he said, standing and putting distance between them. However, she followed and stood too close for comfort.

"And when we reach our destination? What of my skin? What will you do with it?"

Promise me. If you find another way, you must take it. His mother's words rang in his ears. Loud. Incessant.

He avoided eye contact and took yet another step away. "I will keep it to ensure the safety of my clan. Once Oswald's bride, you will not attack us lest you risk harm to your seal skin."

Mayla's nostrils flared. Faster than he thought possible, she lifted her hand and moved to strike him, but he caught her wrist before her palm made contact with his cheek.

Tears trailed down her face, and the sight tied his stomach in knots. Guilt moved through him, pinching and prodding and biting.

"I hope Lise is worth it," she whispered. "I hope she is worth staining your heart black."

Klaus dropped her wrist and turned away, unable to look her in the eye. This was the right thing to do. Not only to salvage his pride, but to send a message that no one could steal their women without dire consequences. But most of all, to keep his family safe.

Without a word, he strode out of the barn, leaving her behind, and ignored the way her seething glare seemed to burn holes in the back of his tunic. The selkie was a means to an end. Nothing more. And definitely not worth feeling guilt or regret over.

The oranges, yellows, and pinks in the sky became tinged with navy blue as the dusk wore on. After collecting his belongings, he ventured toward the sea with his mother, sister, and several other members of the clan. Lise's father and brothers also joined him on the short journey. Between Mayla and Lise's brothers, Klaus felt certain his tunic might fall off completely, tattered from flames of hatred and fury. He had more enemies than he was comfortable with.

They stopped at the edge of the sea where Anders met them. He surreptitiously glanced toward his small *skuldelev* on the shore to find a bundle within. It appeared like a stack of quilts, but if Anders had done as promised, he knew Mayla lay beneath.

A hush gave way to the gentle lapping of water upon the rocks. The salty seawater reached out, matching the yearning inside him, only to pull away in a teasing dance. It had been too long since he'd roamed the sea.

His longing spirit would soon be satiated.

His mother approached with a wooden bowl filled with black paint and dipped her finger in the substance. She painted several lines over one of his eyes with careful precision. "Are you positive you want to leave at dusk?" She continued painting the side of his face with runes. "You won't be able to see."

"And neither will Oswald. He won't see me coming, which will give me the advantage." When the worry remained on her face, he added, "I have sailed these waters dozens of times. I will return unscathed."

His mother took either side of his face and rested her forehead against his as she said her goodbyes. "Bless."

Anders clasped his wrist in farewell, though his worry revealed itself in the downward slant of his eyebrows. "I trust you know what you're doing." He lowered his voice. "But I don't like you going alone."

Equally quiet, he murmured, "I am not alone."

His brother opened his mouth as if to protest but closed it just as quickly and stepped away.

Sten Borgen approached next, hands clenched tight in fists and a tightness in his eyes. "You return with my daughter, or you don't return at all." The man's face crumpled, his voice cracking.

"I don't plan on returning empty handed."

Taking a deep breath, Klaus set his belongings inside the *skuldelev*. The smaller boat with a single sail was meant to be manned by five people in the harsh waters, but he was capable of manning it himself on a calm sea, and he was certain he could enlist Mayla's help if something went wrong.

Between Anders and himself, they pushed the small boat into the ocean, the bottom scraping against rocks and then giving way to the sea. He hopped into the boat before the water could soak his boots.

"Look after Modir and our systirs." He glanced over Anders's shoulder to find Sten with his arms crossed. "The blood feud has not yet ceased without this marriage."

"I will," Anders promised. "May Thor guide your way."

Klaus unfurled the sail, took the oar in his hands, and dipped it into the water, smoothly cutting into the sea with each stroke. Gentle waves buffeted the boat, lifting it up and then back down until he moved farther away from the shore and closer to open waters. Land surrounded him on either side until finally, he found himself far enough away to breathe.

However, his lungs restricted again when he reminded himself he still had a long journey to reach his destination, and when he did, what awaited him would not be pleasant.

His gaze settled on the bundle near his feet. "Mayla, you can come out now."

The bundle shifted, quilts rustling, until a head of brown hair emerged. His chest tightened when he met her gaze, but he tried to shake away the unexpected feelings of attraction and recalled Lise's face. His bride. Lise would be his bride.

From her place on the floor of the boat, she stared back at him for a few moments too long. But then she said, "You look ridiculous with that paint on your face."

Klaus chuckled. "A tradition."

Silence passed between them as she wrestled her skirts while attempting to sit on the seat across from him. Huffy breaths escaped her mouth at what seemed to be a great undertaking. She smoothed her hair back. "What is this blood feud you mentioned?"

His jaw clenched, and he stared out over dark waters barely lit by the glow of a half moon. For several long beats of the oar, he debated remaining silent. But he decided he would rather have her condescending conversation over heated silence.

"It started innocently, more or less," he began. The steady rhythm of rowing helped level the wide array of emotions churning within him. "Norse courtships are short, but to court publicly without a proposal following soon after is frowned upon. My fadir…" He stopped for a moment to clear his throat. "He was a fierce warrior. No one could best him in combat, and therefore, he was chosen as the chieftain of our clan."

Mayla leaned closer as if engrossed in the story.

He continued. "There was a woman he had his eye on, but she was not considered fit to be the wife of a chieftain." He realized he'd stopped rowing and put more strength behind the next dip of the oar. "She had been a slave twice over. First stolen from a smaller clan during a viking. And again when my fadir led a viking on that clan." Again, he cleared his throat, lost in the memories of the tale he'd heard time and again beside a warm fire. "My fadir fell in love with her." He paused to look Mayla in the eye. "The woman was my modir."

"Then is Lise's family angry that your father married her?" she asked, all contempt and disdain gone from her eyes. At least for now.

"Yes, but that's not the reason for the feud. You see, my fadir had originally promised his hand in marriage to Lise's modir. He broke his promise to marry my modir instead. It was considered an incredible slight to their family."

Swish. Shh. Swish. Shh.

The gentle lullaby of the sea was a balm to his spirit, especially in the face of what was to come. "Our families warred for years, the feud steadily becoming more violent with each child born. In the past three years, we've both sustained unacceptable losses. My fadir. My brodir. Their family lost loved ones as well."

He grunted as he pulled the oar into the boat to give himself a momentary break. Little droplets showered the floor by his feet. A little too much water. He needed to take care to allow more water to drip from it first. "To stop this feuding from going any farther, I am to marry Lise to make restitutions."

A frown pulled her gentle mouth downward. "But it is not your feud. Why should you be the one to fix it?"

Hope clung to her voice as if she was beginning to convince herself that she could change his course and get her skin back.

How wrong she was.

"This is my family. I will not dishonor them by walking away."

A glare snapped back to her expression. He cried out in surprise when the boat tipped precariously onto its side and dunked his entire head in the water. He barely managed to hang onto the sides of the vessel to keep himself from falling in.

When the *skuldelev* righted itself, he sputtered against the water stinging his nostrils and the salt burning his eyes. "Gah!" He glared at her, face dripping and water hacking from his lungs. She sat with her back straight, an unreadable expression on her face. The nerve of that woman! "Never do that again."

She sniffed and turned her head away. "It was worth a try."

Klaus snatched the oar before she thought to attempt the feat again. Thankfully, it hadn't fallen into the water, drifting out to sea and leaving them stranded.

He took in his surroundings. They were sailing through wide open waters, the moon reflecting on the rippling surface of the ocean. Land was now the faintest speck in the distance. Someday soon, he hoped to see home again. And with Lise in the *skuldelev* with him instead of the selkie.

"I don't know much about boats…" Mayla said, her eyebrows pinched. "But I don't think they are meant to hold water."

With a roll of his eyes, he scoffed. "Maybe if you stopped trying to overturn the boat, perhaps there would be no water inside it."

He reached beneath the seat behind him, picked up an empty wooden bucket, and thrust it into her arms. "Make yourself useful, selkie."

She glared at him, but he only frowned at the water now lapping at his feet. Just how much had managed to slip inside?

He shifted positions to avoid soaking his shoes and continued rowing in silence. The only sound was Mayla begrudgingly scooping up water and throwing it over the side of the boat. Out of the corner of his eye, he watched the awkward way she handled the bucket, as if she had rarely held anything while in her human form.

Part of him wondered what else she might be capable of with her magic. If she willed it, could she use it to rid the boat of water?

His curiosity couldn't stop him from asking. "Why do you use the bucket instead of your magic?"

All at once, her movements stilled, and she lifted her head. "I could. But it will likely tire me more than doing it this way. Every feat of magic comes with the cost of energy." Her lower lip trembled the slightest bit, and she glanced away. However, he understood what she didn't speak out loud.

If she used too much magic, she could die.

Water continued to lap at his shoes, and he frowned. "Believe me, it's not enjoyable to sleep with damp blankets. If you could hurry…"

"You could help," she pointed out.

"I'm rowing. But we can switch if you'd like. You might soon realize emptying the boat is far preferable and less strenuous."

Mayla raised her eyebrows, not once breaking eye contact and she scooped up water and slowly dumped it over the side. He chuckled at her small bout of humor.

Klaus eyed her again. He knew very little about selkies. A part of him knew he should keep his mouth shut and not care about her, but he wanted to learn more. "What do you eat?"

"Fish."

"Easy enough. We have dried fish for now, and we can catch more if we need to." He tipped his head, his gaze roaming over her long brown hair, the selkie spots on her cheek, and lingering on the soft curve of her mouth. She was beautiful. "Do you eat it…raw?"

"What other way is there?"

"Oh, Mayla." He smiled and shook his head in bewilderment. "You are missing out on the delicacies of fire-roasted salmon and cod. Remind me to cook for you later. You won't be disappointed."

Awkwardness slipped its unwanted presence onto the boat between them as he reminded himself that he wouldn't have time to cook for her before he handed her over to Oswald. A pinch of regret clenched his jaw.

Once again, his mother's words slipped through his mind. *You are a good man. Oswald is not.*

How could he do this to her? Although they weren't well acquainted, could he really be so heartless as to hand her over to a man who would beat her and more? But if he didn't, how many more family members would he lose to the blood feud?

He ignored the guilt prodding into his side like a sharp knife and returned to his task of rowing.

But he paused when the frigid ocean water seeped into his shoes.

He inhaled sharply and glanced down at his feet, only to find more water than previously. Of course, he was heavier than Mayla, which could possibly result in all of the water collecting near him. That and—

"Like I said before," she started slowly, pointing to something near the stacked quilts, now laden with water, "I'm no master of boats, but that hole looks deliberate."

"Hole?" he squeaked.

He threw his oar down and rocked the boat with his desperate attempt to cross the space between them. A wave knocked into the boat just enough for him to lose his balance and fall into Mayla. His face and neck heated as he gazed into her dark eyes, but he pushed away from her and forced his attention away, trying to ignore his fluster as he spotted the place where she pointed.

Sure enough, a small, perfectly rounded hole lay at the base of the *skuldelev*. Large enough to sink the boat. But small enough to sink it when it reached open waters.

Someone had placed the hole on purpose.

He snatched the bucket from Mayla and began scooping water out as fast as possible. But the more water he threw out, the more that returned with a vengeance.

Soon, the water climbed to his ankles despite all of his efforts. In the small space between them, he shared a panicked look with Mayla. The boat was going to sink.

"Is there someone who wishes you harm?" she gasped, now scooping with her hands as he frantically used the bucket beside her. But their efforts were only delaying the inevitable.

"I don't know." Worry gnawed on his bones when he could actually think of *several* people who might wish him harm. Oswald. The witch. Perhaps Lise's family. But he doubted their interference when it would only result in them never seeing Lise again. Not everyone was happy about Klaus becoming the chieftain either. Whoever put the hole in the boat clearly wanted him dead.

He eyed the selkie. "It wasn't you, was it?"

"Me?" she screeched. "I can't swim in this form!"

"Odin's horns, woman! You are supposed to be a seal!"

"Yes, with my *pelt*."

A frustrated growl escaped him. If he didn't think of something and fast, it appeared as if they might both drown before they reached dry land.

He unsheathed his ax and cut strips of cloth from the quilts, and then he stuffed the hole before returning to the task of scooping water out and throwing it overboard.

He breathed heavily from the exertion, perspiration lining his brow. "How long can you hold your breath?" he huffed. "In the event that we may need to abandon ship."

Her voice shook with her answer. "An hour."

"An *hour*? Are you jesting?"

"No. Can't you do the same?"

He chuckled humorlessly as he began to toss things out of the vessel. The blankets went first. Then the fishing net. Followed by several horn bowls and spoons. With a grimace, he threw out his bow and arrows next.

The boat continued to fill with water. Saving it was a hopeless endeavor.

"Listen to me," he said in an intense tone as he grabbed her shoulders and looked into her fearful eyes. The chilly water climbed to his upper ankle, and then his calf. She choked on a sob. "We are going to float on our backs. I will hold onto you the entire time. We are going to survive this."

"How?" she shrieked, unhinging before his eyes. Her chest heaved with each breath. Her gaze darted around the vast ocean surrounding them. Her hands trembled as she clutched onto his arms hard enough to leave fingernail prints in his skin. Even worse, the sea seemed to react to her emotions. Lifting and crashing and swaying. A fierce wind kicked up, spraying him with salty water as sharp as stinging needles.

If she was this panicked *inside* the boat, she would not survive *outside* it. He had to calm her down.

He took her face between his hands to keep her gaze on him rather than their impending predicament. For a moment, the softness of her skin jumbled his thoughts into a foggy stupor. And her eyes… A beautiful shade of brown.

"Stop it!" he grumbled. "Bewitching me is not going to save us."

"I don't have that sort of magic!" Her breaths came faster as her hysteria continued to build. Another wave crashed into the sinking boat, submerging more of the vessel in water.

After successfully shaking off his stupor, he said, "If the sea takes you down, you hold your breath. Understand?" The water now lapped at his knees. One end of the boat dipped beneath the surface. He tossed his ax into the sea, knowing the weight would kill him if he kept it on his person. He tucked a single knife into his boot. "If you can use your magic, then—"

The ocean claimed the rest of the boat in a sudden, unexpected pull. He gasped as frigid water climbed to his neck. He fought to keep his head above the surface when the waves buffeted him as they grew larger and more unforgiving.

Mayla screamed.

Klaus spun around to find water spraying up around her as she kicked and splashed. True terror lived in her eyes. His heart pounded with his own fear, but he held it at bay as he slipped his arm around her waist.

"Mayla!" he shouted but regretted opening his mouth when seawater entered. He choked on it, his eyes burning. "Flip onto your back—"

She clawed at him as if desperate to keep herself from slipping beneath the water, but she only managed to dunk him under as well. He kicked with all his might, fighting to keep them both above the tempest.

His head broke the surface just as a wave crashed over him and pushed him down again. For a moment, he lost his grip on the selkie, and through his blindness, he swiveled in each direction while reaching with his hands. Alarm bubbled in his throat when he couldn't find her.

He couldn't lose her.

Not like this.

Not like this!

When his fingers brushed against hair, he lunged forward and caught her around the shoulders. Before he managed to kick them to the surface once more, something slammed into the back of his head.

And his world turned dark.

CHAPTER 4

Mayla knew something was amiss the moment Klaus became slack against her. Despite the panic clawing at her lungs, despite the fear and the terror of drowning in this form, she forced herself to relax. To hold her breath.

To open her eyes.

The dark skies made it difficult to see beneath the water, but her selkie eyes quickly adjusted and she made out Klaus's features in the murky ocean. His hair floated above his head. His body was limp, and his eyes closed. He was unconscious. Had he breathed in water?

She spotted the boat's oar getting tossed about beneath the sea, and when it ventured closer, she grabbed onto it with one hand while holding tight to Klaus with her free arm. Several moments passed before another wave pulled them back up to the surface. She gasped in air and tried her best to position the man so his airway was clear. He hacked and coughed and sputtered.

But remained unconscious.

Indecision warred in her mind. If she let go, he would surely drown, and then she would be free of him and could possibly retrieve her skin without his interference.

But as she gazed at his unconscious face, at the vulnerability he possessed with his eyes closed, she knew she couldn't. Her conscience refused to let him die.

The tempest calmed a fraction, but holding onto the oar *and* Klaus proved to be difficult, especially when the oar kept dunking under the water beneath their combined weight and the extra weight of their clothing and shoes. In her selkie tongue, she screamed for help.

Darkness swept across the ocean in the form of a thunderous wave, and once more, she found herself submerged in the one place she had always found comfort and solace. How could she have been so foolish as to deny her human form the strength and resilience it needed to survive?

Her hand slipped on the oar, and for a moment, she found herself spiraling in the water as a wave rolled over them. She squeezed her eyes shut and wrapped herself around Klaus to prevent him from getting ripped away from her. Legs around his waist, arms around his shoulders. Fingers barely holding onto what was left of her grip on the oar. Although she could hold her breath for an hour, he clearly didn't possess the same ability. She needed to get him air.

Focus! she internally shouted at herself, and finally, her magic found footing in her frantic heart. It bubbled up inside her, growing hotter and hotter until it released as a *whoosh* from her body.

What felt like an invisible force tugged them forward beneath the water. She willed it to push them to the surface, and just as Klaus had told her, she flipped onto her back beneath him, holding his head steady on her shoulder as her magic pulled them.

Far too soon, exhaustion wore her thin, especially when she found them stranded in the waters once more. She had no idea where to find land. From her vantage point, she could see nothing but darkness and ocean, not a speck of land in sight.

"Wake up!" she sobbed, smacking Klaus in the face. He still breathed. At least, she thought he did. It was difficult to tell. But he didn't wake. "I can't do this without you!"

She pinched his cheek. Nothing.

And then she noticed the dark red mingling with the water around them. Blood.

Her first thought turned to panic. *Sharks.* Her second thought turned to worry. *Klaus.*

Something slick touched her leg and she involuntarily shrieked, kicking against what she feared was a shark. The creature touched her leg again, and she braced herself for a painful bite.

However, none came.

Instead, a brown head with whiskers popped out of the water and barked at her. Not just any seal. Her sister.

"Aislee!" she cried, and she might have thrown her arms around her sister if she wouldn't have lost her hold on Klaus and the oar in the process.

"You have a human," Aislee said in their tongue. *"Drop him so I might take you away."*

She shook her head. "Help us get to land. He's injured."

Her sister stared at her for a long moment, but she must have noticed the pleading in her eyes because she ducked beneath the water and positioned herself under her arm. Several more seals bobbed out of the water, surrounding them, lifting her weary body and Klaus's limp form.

Shaky laughter relaxed her aching muscles as she allowed the seals to propel them forward. It wasn't long before she spotted the dark silhouette of land in the distance. Slowly, it grew larger and larger until she made out the small island.

The seals pushed them as far onto land as they were able. Finding purchase on wet sand, Mayla dropped the oar on the shore and attempted to drag Klaus the rest of the way, grunting with the effort of lifting her heavy clothing and his limp body. He was dense. As if every bit of him was built with solid muscle.

When her muscles could not endure any more agony, she collapsed beside him, breathing heavily. Unfortunately, she did not get enough reprieve before Aislee's head came into view, the dark sky a backdrop to her seal form.

"Mayla, you cannot take a human lover. You saw what happened to Erianna."

A knife stabbed her gut at the reminder of her sister. She had not yet time enough to mourn her death. "He is not my lover. He—" She paused, wincing at the idea of telling her sister the entire truth. Aislee would kill Klaus, and for some deranged reason, she didn't want to see him dead. Nearly drowned, unconscious, and bleeding, Aislee didn't seem to notice Klaus was the same man who had threatened her seal skin. That, or she hadn't gotten a good look at him that day.

"He is not my lover," she tried again, pushing herself into a sitting position despite the intense ache in her body. She turned Klaus's head to inspect his wound. It bled through his hair and onto the sand, but it didn't appear as terrible as she previously thought. How was she supposed to treat it? As a selkie, she healed fairly quickly. But what about humans?

Aislee nudged her arm with her nose. *"Where is your skin? Did the sea claim it? Tell me, and I will go search for it."*

A selkie whine climbed her throat as she found herself torn, trapped between two things she wanted—her freedom and Klaus's life.

Her freedom mattered more.

She moved away from Klaus and dipped her toes into the waxing and waning sea, sighing at the comfort and familiarity of the cool water. Despite nearly drowning, she still longed to return to it. "The humans stole it. I don't know where it is or how to get it back."

Aislee bared her teeth and growled. *"How much will these humans make us suffer? Wake this human man. We will threaten his life if necessary to get him to tell us where it is."*

It was what they *should* do, but it hadn't worked when she'd attempted it before. And that was when he'd held it in his hands.

"Violence will not work with this one."

"Then what will?"

Mayla swallowed and glanced over her shoulder at his limp form. "I don't know."

He groaned, and the sound alone created a pit of worry in her chest. The pit grew larger by the moment until she felt like her ribs might break with the pressure. She hated this feeling. The barbarian man was her enemy. Not her friend.

"I will think of something," she promised. "But I advise you to leave. I don't want you suffering the same fate."

Aislee paused, her black eyes hesitant and uncertain. But she didn't depart without trying to convince her one last time. *"Leave with me. We will find your skin without his help."*

Help. She snorted at the word. But then sobered at the thought of finding her skin in a village filled with humans, with many types of livestock, fields, and buildings. Even if she managed to find her seal skin, she could not do so without getting caught. It was a hopeless cause.

"This is the only way."

"I don't like this."

"Neither do I." She grimaced when Klaus groaned again. "Hurry. Go! Do not come back. The next time we see each other, it will be because I find you."

Thankfully, Aislee simply nodded and splashed into the surf. With a kick of her flippers, she disappeared beneath the water. A sense of loss took hold of her and squeezed. She would see her sister again. She had to believe it.

Mayla turned to find Klaus blinking sluggishly at his surroundings before his eyes found hers in the waning darkness. "You," he coughed weakly, "are the worst swimmer I have ever met."

She huffed. "I should have let you drown." But as she attempted to stalk toward him, she tripped on the hem of her dress and crashed onto the gritty sand.

A weak chuckle. "And you are terrible at walking, too."

She fought against her skirts and lost, sitting back on her heels and rubbing her hands up and down her arms to try to regain some of the warmth she'd lost to the ocean. "I hate you."

"The feeling is mutual."

But as she gazed into his blue eyes, now closer in proximity than moments before, she realized something had changed. She was worried about him, which proved her words were a lie. This wasn't right. To care for a human to any degree would only end badly.

The man tipped his head to the side and hissed.

"Stop moving," she ordered, freeing her legs enough to seat herself next to him. "You are only making it worse."

Another moan, followed by a shiver. "What happened?"

"I think the oar hit you. Or the boat. I'm not entirely sure." With gentle fingers, she placed her hands on either side of his face and closed her eyes.

"What are you—"

"Shh."

Concentrating her magic within her core, she allowed it to pool within herself before gently coaxing it through her body. It traversed through her veins, up her arms, and then escaped as a soft silver light through her hands. She allowed her healing power to seep into Klaus, and as if starving, his body eagerly latched onto it.

The wound on his head began to knit closed, the gash becoming a cut, the cut becoming a scratch, until it disappeared altogether. All that remained was a scar beneath his hairline. Next, she focused her magic on their clothing until little by little, their damp clothes dried completely.

Her silver light faded into nothing. Exhaustion caused her shoulders to slump, fatigue pressing down on her with the feat.

Klaus's breath hitched as he sat up straight, his fingers probing the back of his head. "It's…it's gone." His attention snapped to her. "You healed me? Why would you…"

His words trailed off, a frown forming as he slowly shook his head. For a few long moments, he stared into her eyes as if trying to seek answers from the brief contact of their souls, from her essence slowly slipping from his body.

"I need...I need some air," he gasped. And despite fresh air all around them, he picked himself up off the sand and ventured farther away. She watched as he located several rocks and tree branches of different sizes, and he tore the leaves from the trees into large strips. He then sat on a boulder, smashing the rocks together until flecks flew in all directions, creating a sharp point.

An arrowhead.

She'd seen humans use such weapons to hunt for fish in streams and in shallow water. The process of making such a weapon fascinated her.

When he tied the sharp rocks to the branches with the strips of leaves, he kicked off his shoes, rolled his trousers up to his knees, entered the shallow water up to his calves, and paused. Waiting patiently. So still that she wasn't sure he was breathing.

She cocked her head to the side, watching him in the dim light from the moon. During the times she'd studied humans, she had come to the conclusion that they couldn't see in the dark. Yet, Klaus perplexed her. Was he proving her wrong?

In a movement faster than a flash of lighting, he thrust his weapon into the water.

And missed.

It seems I am right, she thought to herself. *He cannot see in the dark.*

Although her body felt almost too numb and fatigued to move, she climbed to her feet, now bare after losing her shoes to the ocean, and wrestled with her infuriating skirts as she approached. One foot into the water. And then another.

"You are going to soak your clothing again," Klaus cautioned. "You must first gird up your loins."

She paused, the hem of her dress brushing the water. "I don't know what that means."

He clenched his jaw. "Do *not* make me do it for you."

She glanced from his distressed eyes to his flared nostrils, and then to her skirt. Although she didn't understand his words, she had a vague understanding. The human man seemed extremely uncomfortable with her nakedness. Among selkies, it did not matter, as they never wore human clothing. But she would respect his wishes, nonetheless.

Mouth twitching back and forth with pondering, she slowly did as he instructed step by step by pulling the end of her skirt up to her knees, between her legs, and tucked it in her belt in the front. Klaus's jaw clenched again, his gaze roaming over her legs but then quickly darting away. But not without a flush climbing the back of his neck.

Uncomfortable? she asked herself, heart racing. *Or something else?*

After picking up a second spare spear from where it rested against the boulder, she joined him in the water, both patiently holding still. "Why are you not waiting to fish when you can see?" she murmured, not daring to move a muscle.

"Because I can't *do* anything else!" He grimaced at the volume of his voice. "We're stuck on land with no boat and only four snot-nosed days left to reach our destination. And I'm frustrated because there is nothing I can do about it!" He slapped at the water with his hand, but then winced with what appeared to be regret for scaring the fish away. "So I'm out here, fishing blindly because it's the only thing I can do."

Klaus dipped his head, jaw clenched, stress lines around his eyes.

"I don't have my whiskers for hunting…" she said slowly, "But I can see in the dark."

"Can you?" Surprise lit his features, and he turned more fully toward her. "And can you properly use a spear?"

The last thing she wanted to do was catch dinner in her exhausted state, but what else could she do to help?

She grinned and smacked him on the back of the knee with the blunt end of the branch, which effectively brought out a faint smile of his own. "Well enough. It's a bit slower doing it this way, but I'm sure I'll manage."

"Slow?" He laughed. "Pray do tell. How fast can you catch a fish in your seal form, selkie?"

"Faster than you, to be sure."

They stood close to each other in the moonlight, her stomach tying itself in knots beneath his intense stare. Her gaze roamed over his messy hair, handsome face, and lingered on his lips. Heat smoldered in her belly, and she stiffened in surprise. The human man was not a selkie, and he kept her pelt captive in a secret place. Yet, feelings of attraction and desire danced within her chest.

Her mouth snapped closed as she clammed up, her attention returning to his eyes.

As if unaware of her shift in feelings, he smiled, gently poked her in the side with the blunt end of his own spear, and then moved past her. The water swished around his legs until he reached the sand, and then his footsteps became muffled.

"If you can manage, I will build a fire. We'll need it to get through the rest of the night."

She watched him, noticing the way his shirt clung to the broad muscles of his arms and chest. His rolled-up pants exposed nicely toned legs and an even firmer—

Her face flamed as she pulled her gaze away. She could not afford to ogle him when she needed to convince him to return her skin. Preferably without threats, bloodshed, or trickery.

But she would do what she had to in the end.

CHAPTER 5

Anders Lovik stood on the shore, watching his brother leave with the selkie aboard his boat. Worry gnawed on his stomach, churning it until he became nauseous. Even with the great powers of the selkie on his side, facing Oswald was a terrible idea. Klaus should have an entire fleet at his command, waging war against Oswald's clan, fighting for what was theirs, and coming out victorious.

Behind him, his mother gasped. With furrowed brows, he turned, only to freeze when he felt the cold blade of a knife pressed against his throat. A knife also rested against his mother, one of the Borgen brothers threatening her life with the small weapon. Her eyes were big, round spheres pooled with fear and submission. She was a strong woman. But considering her past…

He must protect her at all costs.

"Why are you doing this?" he growled. "The contract—"

"—is void." Sten's voice came directly behind him. "It was never meant to be fulfilled."

He squeezed his fists hard enough for his knuckles to crack. "You dirty, cheating, rotten—"

The knife pressed closer, and he immediately shut his mouth.

"Your brodir is as good as dead," Sten hissed in his ear. "Lay down your weapons. I am the new chieftain."

Clenching his jaw, Anders untied his sword from his belt and tossed it onto the rocks, quickly followed by his knives. A man stepped forward and scooped them up. Sten continued to hold him captive with the weapon.

"Release my modir," Anders commanded. "She is innocent in our feud."

"No Lovik is innocent. My wife is gone. Your family has wronged her in many ways." The man's voice lowered dangerously. "Her death will not be for naught."

Sten nodded toward his son, who held his mother at knifepoint. "Keep her as our captive for now. Once the people have accepted me as the new chieftain, every Lovik will die."

As one of the Borgen brothers began dragging his weeping mother away, Anders elbowed Sten hard in the ribs, causing him to drop his knife. He spun around, drew back a fist, and smashed his knuckles into the man's face.

But moments later, several men jumped on him and pinned him down with his face crushed into the ground. He bucked and writhed, fighting against those who restrained him but to no avail.

"May Odin punish you for your deception!" Anders spat. "When I kill you, there will be no honor left for you."

Sten stepped on his fingers, and he withheld a cry of pain. "The only honor will be mine when I cut out your throat and feed it to my dogs." He signaled with his hand. "Tie him up. I want him where everyone can see his ugly hide."

Anders fought against the scratchy restraints. Though, with multiple men against only himself, he lost the battle. He cast one last glance toward his mother's silhouette in the distance. He vowed to himself he would find a way out of this.

And when he made a vow, he never broke it.

CHAPTER 6

Klaus could not believe his eyes.

From where she stood in the water, Mayla triumphantly held up her spear in the darkness, three fish skewered on the branch, flapping and flopping in a fruitless attempt to escape. Her joyous laughter lifted into the skies, her smile bright enough to rival the moon. His heart pattered in his chest, warm and unexpected and not entirely unwelcome.

The woman was endearing. Even the strongest willed of men would have a hard time resisting her unique charm.

She trudged through the water in his direction, where a fire now billowed to life on the sand.

But she tripped over her own foot and shrieked before the sea swallowed the sound as she went under.

"Mayla!" he gasped, launching to his feet. However, her head broke the surface, hair drenched and a pretty scowl on her face. She finished her laborious journey out of the water and slumped onto the beach, now dripping from head to toe. Like before, silvery magic weaved around her and dried her clothing. He watched transfixed as the water stopped dripping from her skirts, transitioning to semi-damp threads, and then dried completely with a faint flutter of a breeze wafting over the hem of her sark.

He opened his mouth, but no sound escaped. Selkies were incredible. More so than he'd imagined, and he'd only witnessed two small miracles.

Find another way…

A shuddering breath left his lips. What other way was there?

But the thought of the hurt and betrayal on Mayla's face when he traded her for Lise stung. *If* they managed to escape the island, he knew witnessing her inevitable anger would hurt.

Slowly, she pulled one fish off the spear, and then another, handing each to him. "Have I ever mentioned how infuriating this body is?"

"It's infuriating just watching you try to manage it," he jested. He expected a glare, but the amused look he received instead surprised him. "You will get used to it. It will only take time."

He turned away from her to gut the fish and placed them on a heated rock over the blazing fire. The rock released a satisfying sizzle, but when he faced her again, his eyes snapped open in shock when she clamped her teeth on the remaining fish, its tail flipping wildly in protest against her chin.

"Ah, no! That is not how you eat it."

She stared at him with wide, innocent eyes, the fish continuing to wriggle in her mouth.

Not able to help himself, he burst into laughter. The sound grew louder, and he doubled over when she pulled the fish out of her mouth, revealing the giant tooth-marked chunk missing from it.

"This is how I always eat," she protested. "How else would I consume it?"

He took what remained of her raw meal, gutted it, and placed it next to the others on the heated rock. "You will never want it raw again. I promise you."

The smell of cooked fish wafted into the air, teasing his nostrils. His stomach rumbled with hunger, making him realize just how long he'd gone without food.

Or water.

All of the blood drained from his face, humor fleeing from him altogether. They would not last long on this island without fresh water to drink. Could he possibly find a way to signal to his clan for help? A large bonfire, perhaps? Would they be able to see it? He could barely make out the dark speck of his homeland from the island. It was far enough to not only strand him but make communication difficult if not impossible.

Perhaps the only way to escape death was to survive long enough for someone to sail by on their ship. But by then, too many days would have passed, and Oswald would have claimed Lise as his own bride.

He sat with his legs pulled to his chest, staring into the dancing and burning flames as he twisted his wedding band around his finger. It was a hoax of a symbol to represent what had not yet transpired. Seconds! He had been seconds away from claiming the woman as his wife. And now he worried over his family. Would something happen in his absence? Would the Borgen family seek justice and attempt to take their lives?

"You are quiet," Mayla murmured. "And not just in your normal brooding sort of way."

Klaus didn't react to her teasing barb, but instead continued to stare into the fire with a focused gaze and hands clasped together. The question burning through his mind ate at him: What next?

"You saved my life."

Out of the corner of his eye, he saw her shrug. "After I put it at risk, I suppose… I am sorry I could not swim."

"Not all women can."

"But I should be able to. I'm a selkie."

"A selkie who is clearly unused to using her human form." He turned his head and rested his cheek on his knee. "I don't fault you. It's not by your doing that we're here."

Her nostrils flared as if picking apart the scents of the cooking fish. He scraped one of them off the heated rock and transferred it to a cool rock, handing it to her. She inspected it, sniffed it, and licked it with the tip of her tongue.

"Stop that," he chuckled, nudging her with his foot. "Just eat it."

"It's hot." Her nose wrinkled with dissatisfaction. "Fish are not meant to be hot."

He studied her, tilting his head curiously. "How often did you say you were in your human form?"

"Not often. Mostly to do each other's hair, to collect shells, to take lovers."

He clenched his jaw so hard that it ached, putting more force than necessary into tearing the meat of the fish from the skin and grinding it against his teeth as he chewed. He hardly tasted it.

"Huh," she said after a minute, and he glanced over to find her biting through the fish, skin and all. "I like this. It's flaky and surprisingly flavorful."

"Better than its raw counterpart?"

The selkie shook her head. "I can't say it's better, but I do like it plenty enough."

With a roll of his eyes, he grinned and rubbed the back of his head. He sure found her adorable.

But the action reminded him of his previous wound. The wound he had not yet expressed his appreciation for her healing. "Thank you," he said slowly. "For what you did earlier. I knew you possessed great power, but I didn't realize you could heal as well."

"It was only a small wound." She shrugged, moving her attention to the sand wriggling beneath her fingers. "Now if it were something that might have threatened your life, it would have been more difficult."

"How so?"

She paused as if pondering her next words, as if debating if she could trust him with the information. "My magic is…wild. To heal a fatal wound, I would need a great deal of magic. But without something to contain it, to channel it, it could have catastrophic consequences. Like—"

"—drowning an entire island?"

She grimaced. "Yes. Something of that sort."

"And…" He spoke slowly, eyebrows furrowed together. "What would happen to you for attempting such a feat?"

Another shrug. She trailed her finger through the sand, creating glyphics completely foreign to him. Foreign but beautiful with a range of swirls, dots, and symbols. "Death, if we allow our magic to run wild. With it contained, perhaps we would lose our magic altogether, or even our ability to shift." She chuckled nervously. "But no selkie would ever sacrifice their seal form. Nothing is worth losing it."

Her posture stooped, and her features pulled into a melancholy expression. A lump of regret formed in his throat, difficult to swallow.

He changed the subject, pointing to the glyphics visible beneath the flickering firelight. "What are those?"

She resumed her drawing. "It's how selkies communicate in writing. This means 'sisterly bond.'" She smiled, adding several more lines and dots. "And if I add a little more to it, it means 'true love.' There is no truer love than that of sisters."

"Then have you never been in love?"

Mayla snapped her head up, meeting his gaze. Shadows moved across her face, and the firelight accentuated the faint sheen in each of her eyes, similar to that of an animal's. He briefly wondered if the abnormality helped her see in the dark.

"Have you?" she countered as if avoiding his question.

He twisted the ring around his finger again. "I fancied myself in love a few times in my youth. It was nothing more than inconsequential relationships, secret trysts, and avoiding getting trapped in an unwanted feud and especially an unwanted marriage. But my parents...I have witnessed no love truer than theirs."

A soft smile spread across his face as he recalled their laughter, joyful smiles, and constant wooing. With his finger, he drew out the symbols in his own language. "These are runes in my tongue that have a similar meaning. 'True love', they read." He finished off the last symbol with a final straight line. "My modir used to say there was no magic greater than true love. But after witnessing what you are capable of with magic, I'm not so sure she was correct."

"You said you fancied yourself in love in your youth," she said slowly, glancing at him beneath her lashes. "Do you not love Lise?"

The ring on his finger seemed to tighten, squeezing the life out of it. His secret hope, his inner desires… They all burned to ash at his feet. "Not everyone gets a happy beginning like my parents. Perhaps not even a happy ending. My job is to protect my family. My clan. Love has nothing to do with my duty."

She remained quiet after his non-declaration, and he glanced up, only to find her yawning through a shiver. She hugged her arms closer to herself, and when she yawned again, he watched as she laid down with a weary slump.

Exhausted from the long day's events, he laid down beside her. There was nothing more he could do until he could see. First thing in the morning, he planned to seek out a source of fresh water.

Mayla's teeth began chattering.

"You are shivering," he commented.

"I find the weather much colder in this form."

He turned onto his side, head propped up by his hand. "This is much more bearable than the winter months. We often have to resort to sharing beds to keep warm in the worst of the weather."

She wrinkled her nose. "Why would you do that?"

"I'll show you why."

However, when he reached for her, she flinched away. "I will not be your concubine."

He breathed in deeply and let it out slowly to regain some of his patience. "I have never once wanted that of you. You are freezing. If you want to be miserable the remainder of the night, go right ahead. But if you don't, then you will have to share my body heat."

Suspicion continued to lurk in Mayla's eyes. "I will drown you if you try anything."

His mouth twitched as he tried holding back his jest, but he couldn't in the end. "To this day, you have tried it twice and threatened it a few more times. I think you are incapable of drowning me."

And then he flinched, bracing himself for the inevitable. But when it didn't come, he cracked his eyes open to find her raising a brow at him.

"Why are you flinching?"

"You aren't going to splash me with water?"

"Should I?"

The tension melted from his shoulders, and his smile made an appearance as he relaxed. "No, I suppose—"

Out of nowhere, a stream of water hit him in the face. He coughed and sputtered, sneezing once when it tickled his nose. "Gah! You awful creature!" He swiped a hand through his wet hair. "You wound me."

He turned away with his back to her. All of the women in his life seemed to enjoy bashing his pride with a hammer until it lay in pieces at his feet. Of course, it wasn't Lise's fault but rather Oswald's. And then Mayla... Perhaps he deserved her disdain.

Why did the thought bother him?

A gentle hand touched his back, and he inhaled sharply, his shoulders becoming stiff. Slowly, he turned just enough to see the uncertainty in Mayla's eyes. A strand of her dark hair fell over her face, almost hiding the attractive way she bit her bottom lip, not seeming to realize what the simple action did to him. His heart fluttered unexpectedly, his pulse roaring through his ears.

"I would like to share your body heat," she whispered.

The tips of his ears burned as his gaze dropped once more to her lips. "Don't speak in such a manner."

"What manner?"

Another deep breath filled his lungs with a desire for patience. "Nothing. Come here. Move closer."

He helped position her so their bodies were flush against each other, her head resting on his arm and one of her legs pinned between his. Her bare foot brushed against his ankle, which sent an unexpected wave of fiery longing through him.

Now was not the time to be entertaining such thoughts.

In the several moments of silence that passed, he feared she might be able to hear his heart trying to break free of his chest. The wavy strands of her hair tickled his cheek like a gentle caress, and her fingers absently played with the fabric of his sleeve. He was aware of every point where they touched and her sweet exhales brushing against his chin. Her scent wafted from her and teased his nostrils. Seawater with a faint trace of a floral aroma.

"Are there selkie men out there?" he blurted, but then cringed at his less-than-subtle execution of his inner ponderings.

Her fingers paused on his sleeve before she tilted her head to look at him. Which put them close enough for his chest to squeeze with tantalizing emotion.

"There are." She tilted her head back more and laughed, eyes glistening with merriment. Her lips curled into a smile. "Are there human women out there?"

"That's not the same thing. I have only heard tales of selkie women. Why?"

As if unaware of her actions, she now traced the neckline of his tunic, which dipped enough to show a portion of his chest. A light coating of sand stuck to the dried clothing. "Perhaps because of the same reason mermaids are spun about in song and poetry. They are beautiful, mysterious people who love attention from sailors." Her fingers brushed against his skin, and the breath froze in his lungs completely. "Selkie women historically are blessed with great powers of the sea. Our men will protect us, hunt for us, and keep us happy."

His eye involuntarily twitched. It sounded as if selkie women were treated like queens, waited on by their men. The thought of her with other men irked him. "Tell me more about these male selkies."

She lifted her head slightly and looked him in the eye. "They are much different than us females. They don't possess the affinity for magic, but they train with weapons, as they spend much more of their time in their human forms than in their selkie skins, which they wear on their backs like a cloak."

"Why?" The next pause spurred his heart into an irregular rhythm when her finger dipped to explore his chest.

"They are next to powerless in their seal forms and formidable opponents with weapons in their hands." She smiled softly as if recalling a memory. "Our males can also be very gentle and loving." Her finger moved to trace his throat. He swallowed hard. "When one male wants a female as his mate, he will present her with a lovely strand of pearls for her to wear as a necklace. I've known several females tempted into forming a permanent mating bond by the quality of the pearls alone."

"Are you attached to someone?" he blurted.

"Attached…" she murmured, brows puckered in thought. Her finger skimmed between his collarbones and drew a circle on his skin. "I don't understand the term in your tongue."

"Are you married?" he clarified. "Receiving attention from male suitors?"

"Oh, in a romantic manner?" Quickly, she snatched her hand away from his chest as if just realizing what she was doing. "I have not yet chosen a mate. If I had, he would have skewered you through the heart before you had a chance to open that irritating mouth of yours."

Yet, as she said those words, she stared at his mouth as if transfixed.

What if… Could he…?

It was a terrible idea.

But he wanted to.

It was almost as if a tingle of magic still remained in his chest, spurring his movements, his desire, his want. Slowly, he lifted his hand, watching for her reaction as he grazed his finger against her cheek. She stilled. But she didn't protest nor move away. He more daringly traced her jaw from ear to chin, and then with his thumb, he caressed the three brown selkie spots he admired so much on her cheekbone. They were different. Interesting. Beautiful. By the stars, she was gorgeous.

The thread on what little control he had snapped. He leaned in closer and gently kissed one of the selkie spots. When he kissed the second spot, she sighed and relaxed into him, pulling herself closer by latching her fingers onto his tunic. But as he kissed the third spot, she inhaled sharply, her eyes wide with distress.

"Do not hurt me!"

He dropped his hands from her face, confused. "I have never hurt you."

"I was not speaking of physically. But now that we're on the subject… You nicked me with your sword upon our first meeting!"

His expression fell into a scowl. "You did that yourself. You would think you would have the good sense to remain still with a weapon against your neck."

"You did not have to place it against me."

"I did not think you would move!"

Mayla huffed and withdrew her hands from him completely. The loss of her heat put a startling fissure through his soul, one he'd had no idea could exist. He wanted her closer. To bridge the separation. To mend the crack.

"The least you could do is apologize." Her lower lip jutted out in an innocent pout.

"For what?" he sputtered, trying to keep up with the conversation when his heart shouted louder than their spoken words.

"Do you really want me to list your misdeeds?" She held up her hand and began counting on her fingers. "You interrupted my sister's funeral and took me away without allowing me to grieve nor put her to rest with a grave marking. You stole my pelt and forced me into these wretched human garments. You carted me off to the sea in this form and nearly made me drown."

"That wasn't me—"

"And what about Lise?" Her voice rose. "Love or not, you are still wearing her ring! You are very much *attached*. Unless you are planning on being disloyal to her behind her back. And I will not be your concubine."

The shouting in his heart ebbed into a somber song. Slow. Melancholy. Full of aching and regret. He absently touched the key hanging from his neck beneath his shirt, the one that would unlock the chest containing her seal skin. He could still give it back and somehow face the danger ahead alone. But he didn't want her to leave, even if they managed to find a way off the island.

The thought of her absence plucked the notes of sadness within his heart, far stronger than it had any right to sing, especially after their short acquaintance. He didn't know why he felt so drawn to the selkie. It made little sense.

In a hoarse whisper, he asked, "What was your sister's name?"

Mayla's chin trembled, and her voice cracked with her words. "Erianna Brior. She was my elder by three years." Tears now fell freely from her eyes. "She chose a human as her mate. He rejected her. Stole the child. The babe died under his care." She began weeping, the sound ripping the crack in his soul wider. "She used too much magic drowning the village. It killed her. And...and..." She swiped at her tears. "I miss her so much."

She sobbed into his chest, and he wrapped both arms around her as she mourned her sister. The confession of Erianna drowning the village came as a shock. So it *hadn't* just been a rumor or an exaggeration. It was an awful thing to have done, but he still sympathized with the sister. He imagined being rejected by someone you loved and then losing a child might destroy a person.

His heart cracked even more for the precious selkie in his arms. So heartbroken. So vulnerable. So different than what he thought he'd find on the beach that day.

And he held her, weeping, until she fell asleep in his arms.

For what felt like the first time in his life, he didn't know what to do. If they ever managed to get off the island, he wasn't sure he could follow through with trading her to Oswald. She deserved better. But how much would he lose by giving her up to the sea?

CHAPTER 7

armth caressed Mayla's face. Warmth and sunshine and happiness. She pictured herself basking on warm rocks, face upturned to sunny skies, and the familiarity of safety encircling her. The salty sea air greeted her nose. Seagulls cried overhead. And the familiar scent of seals surrounded her.

Seals and…something else…

Her nostrils flared as she picked apart the scent of musky fur, the spice of male skin, and the faint trace of campfire. Selkie men didn't smell of fire and smoke but rather of pearls and silt.

Her eyes flew open just as a male voice shouted, "Gah! Get away, you massive, whiskered creatures!"

Klaus batted at the air in front of a curious seal who tried to sniff at his leg. A dozen more seals lay basking in the sun, barking at the commotion he made. Two more approached him from behind, awkwardly dragging themselves across the beach. One more daringly nipped at his arse, and the man actually shrieked.

Laughter bubbled out of her, and she lifted her head to rest on her knuckles as she watched the humorous display. From where he continued swatting at them, he glared at her.

"Don't just lay there. Do your selkie thing!"

"And what is it you think I can do?" She laughed again when one of the seals latched onto his pant leg with its mouth and gave it a good tug, nearly knocking him onto his face. "They're playing. They like you."

Against her better judgement, she found herself liking him as well.

"I don't think mauling a person to death counts as affection."

One of the seals waddled over to her and nudged her chin with its nose before rubbing its head against her to mingle with her scent.

"Are these seals?" he asked hesitantly. "Or selkies?"

She raised an eyebrow at him, now watching as he leaped over one of the creatures to put a boulder between them. "They like you a little *too* much to be selkies. Don't you think?"

His glare intensified. "I'm sure they are only mauling me because I smell like *you*. If I smelled as delicious as you do, I would maul me, too." A seal popped around the boulder and bounded toward him. "Stop! In the name of all things selkie, leave my arse alone." He clambered onto the boulder.

Mayla laughed so hard, tears leaked from her eyes. Through her laughter, she managed to explain, "When a male smells like a female, it gets other female seals interested. They are curious about why a female would choose you as a mate." She grimaced and ran a strand of her hair through her fingers. "Not that I chose you as a mate. But," she cleared her throat, "you know."

"Are you talking about how you cuddled up to me all night?" he teased, but quickly yelped when a seal nipped at him again. "Down, girl! I am not interested in you. Depart from my boulder!" He glanced at her in distress. "Surely, you can use some sort of selkie magic to make them stop."

"I will take pity on you." Although her face still heated from his earlier comment and from the memories of his strong arms wrapped tight around her, she sat up and bared her teeth, allowing a growl to escape her throat. "Mine!" she barked in her selkie tongue. The seals hesitantly backed away but didn't leave him alone completely. She growled again, and in a more serious and possessive tone, she repeated, "Mine."

Each of the seals dejectedly turned away from him and returned to their basking. They steered clear of her, not meeting her eye nor glancing Klaus's way.

"Thank Odin's breath." He hopped down from the boulder and sprayed sand around him when he landed. "What did you tell them?"

"Nothing." She turned away from him as well, face lifting toward the late morning sun and eyes closed as she combed her fingers through her hair. The strands were tangled, but she patiently worked through the mess.

She frowned when a shadow passed over her, blocking out the sunlight. She peeked an eye open to find Klaus standing over her, arms crossed and expression stern. For a moment, she wondered if he would demand to know the truth.

Thankfully, he didn't ask.

"I need to find drinking water. How long can you last without?"

She reached out to his leg and pushed him to the side so the sunlight once again caressed her face. "I don't need it. I consume enough water from the fish I eat."

For a moment, his mouth slackened, but then he raised his eyebrows. "You never cease to surprise me. Then you just stay here while I search the island. Unless you want to help."

He unfolded his arms and dropped them to his sides. She inhaled sharply, a tingle traveling up her body and jolting through her heart when she spotted his bare finger. He no longer wore Lise's ring. Not on his ring finger. Not on *any* finger.

"I…" he started, biting his lip as he hid his hand behind his back. "I'm not sure how long we'll be here. After I find water, I can make us a shelter. It looks like it might rain."

Her attention turned from him to the gray clouds on the horizon, steadily approaching. "How long can you go without water?"

"A few days at most."

"*Days?*" She looked him over from his sturdy shoulders to his muscled arms to his steady stance. "You are a weak little human." Yet, the information worried her.

He rolled his eyes. "Not everyone can hold their breath for an hour and survive solely on fish. I'll see what I can find." And then he pointed to one of the seals. "Hilda, you behave."

A smile appeared on her lips at his humor as she watched his retreating back. But then her smile fell, her stomach knotting. Not once had she seen Klaus drink from his waterskin on the boat, which now likely lay at the bottom of the sea. One day had already passed. He only had two more left.

Distant thunder boomed across the horizon, dragging her attention back to the looming clouds. An idea struck her. If he didn't find fresh water to drink, she would find a way to catch it.

An uncomfortable burning sensation climbed Klaus's dry, parched throat. He licked his lips in an attempt to wet them. It was as if the moisture dried immediately, threatening to crack his lips. He swallowed. The burn remained.

"Flaming daggers!" he shouted to the skies, ducking beneath the branch of a tree and stepping over protruding roots. "No boat. No water. No shelter. Klaus, you are very good at muddling things."

In his frustration, he kicked the trunk of a tree, only to wince when pain shot up his leg. In his fatigued state, hardly enough energy remained to continue forward. He slumped onto a root that jutted out of the ground at an awkward angle, shoulders hunched as he massaged his temples.

There was no denying it. Someone had tried to kill him.

And he would have died if it hadn't been for Mayla—the one person who should have let him drown but didn't. His would-be killer might still be successful if he didn't manage to find water.

"Who would attempt such a thing?" he rasped to himself, staring out over layers of leafy green trees, mounds of earth, and the sparkling ocean peeking out from between thick trunks. "Even worse, how could I let my guard down so thoroughly?"

He released a sigh and grabbed the cord around his neck, pulling it out from beneath his shirt until the two objects it strung clacked together.

A key.

And his wedding band.

Promise me. If you find another way, you must take it.

Over the last couple of days, his mother's words had buried its roots deep within his soul and flowered.

His conscience no longer allowed him to wear the ring on his finger. In his heart, he knew he couldn't renew the marriage contract with Lise. It was a hard decision, one he did not make lightly, but he would not marry the woman when his heart stirred for another. He dared to think perhaps he could marry someone else…

At the thought, he climbed to his feet with what little determination he could muster and scoured the island. It wasn't large, and after an hour of fruitlessly searching for water, he gave up. A brisk wind began to pick up as the storm moved closer yet danced just out of reach. The mist of rainfall fell across the horizon. Teasing. Tantalizing. Perhaps a punishment from the gods.

"I made a mistake," he murmured to the skies as he prayed to Freyr, the god of rain. "I never should have captured her. I never should have stranded her here with me."

A rumble of thunder moved from one end of the dark clouds to the other. The rain continued to evade him.

"Please," he begged. "Give us water. Give us a way to save ourselves."

More thunder. But through his weary eyes, it seemed as if the storm moved away from him rather than toward. He no longer had the gods' favor, and it was his own doing. How could he possibly make this right?

He fingered the key hanging from his necklace with one hand while holding his churning stomach with the other. Fear and doubt whispered in his ear. If he gave Mayla the key to retrieve her seal skin, would she leave him? Race to the sea and never return?

If he gave her what she wanted, would he lose the one person he desired?

He bit his lip as he hid the key beneath his shirt once more.

"Klaus."

He jumped at the sound of his name and spun around to find Mayla doubled over, breathing hard. He peered behind her at the short journey from the beach to his location and frowned. "I insist you spend more time in your human form." Gesturing to all of her, he added, "This cannot be good for your well-being."

She winced as she straightened. "I dislike this form. It's weak and clumsy."

Raising an eyebrow, he fought back a chuckle. "Likely because you have not spent enough time out of your skin. Besides, I think this form is beautiful."

Her body turned rigid, followed by a blush staining her cheeks. His palms began to perspire at his confession of attraction, and he bit his cheek as he wondered how she might react. He knew he did not deserve her affection. But he wanted it all the same.

"You are certainly no selkie yourself," she said, running her fingers through her hair, "but I suppose you are also pleasing to the eye."

His heart skipped in his chest, and his mouth flickered with a smile. A small triumph. At least until the first half of her sentence sank in. He scoffed. "Is that right? What will it take to impress you then?"

When he sat on a fallen branch and patted the space beside him, she lowered herself and stared at him cautiously.

"May I?" he asked without giving her a chance to answer. He gestured to one of her bare feet, and after she nodded, he picked up her foot and grimaced. Like the day before, blisters formed on her skin from the tips of her toes to her heel. It was a miracle she could still walk. "What happened to your shoes?" He gently inspected each blister, tenderly cradling her foot.

"I must have lost them when the boat sank."

He lifted his head and studied her face. Dark circles lined her eyes. Worry knotted her brow. The corners of her mouth were pinched with pain. All her suffering was his doing.

He brushed his fingers against her soft cheek and whispered, "Forgive me." His mouth closed, unable to finish the sentence when there was so much to forgive.

Her lips parted, and she glanced back and forth between his eyes as if in search of something.

After setting her foot down, he slapped his knees and stood. Words were nothing without actions. Although he didn't know if she would ever forgive him for all of his wrongdoings, he wanted to take care of her and earn her trust. Starting now.

"We need a shelter, and you," he gestured to the whole of her, "need some rest. Sit here. Stay off your feet. This likely won't take too long."

He got to work by stripping large pieces of rotted bark off dying trees and placed them into a pile. Next to the bark, he dragged branches and dead trees roughly the same size. He also managed to find leaves a similar width as his head and separated them into long ribbons.

When he felt a pair of eyes on him, he turned to find Mayla watching him from where she sat. His heart beat erratically in his chest, and he tried to ignore her watchful gaze as he stacked the trees and branches against each other, tying them together with the sturdy leaves where they crossed. Then, he secured the large pieces of bark over the branches to act as shingles to protect them from the coming rain.

Standing with his fists resting on his hips, his chest rising and falling from rapid, labored breaths, he studied the opening to the shelter. It needed a door. And some sort of bedding to lie on.

But he was so tired.

And so thirsty.

Yet, he trekked on, pushing himself even when he wanted to collapse. He managed to find a couple more large pieces of bark to use as a door and gathered up a pile of leaves for bedding. When he finished, he stood back to admire his handiwork. The shelter wasn't perfect, but it would do the job for now.

Mayla approached, placed a hand on his arm, and gazed into his eyes, saying nothing with her words yet speaking with her eyes alone. He felt her sincere gratitude and dare he think it, even fondness for him. The idea solidified when she squeezed his arm. Her fingers trailed down to his wrist, his hand, his fingers, until she released him and entered the shelter. The touch spurred his pulse into a frenzy, and for several beats too long, he stared after her.

When he finally turned away, he released a long breath and made his final decision. He had found another way. And he swore to see it through.

CHAPTER 8

Klaus longingly stared out over the horizon the next morning. The sheet of falling rain still lingered, and with it fresh, crisp air blew into his face. Yet the storm continued to evade them.

He licked his dry lips and swallowed against what felt like sand in his throat. His gaze traveled from the dark clouds toward the speck of his homeland in the distance. So close but still too far.

A painful rumble squeezed his stomach, reminding him of his incessant hunger. Like the rainfall, fish evaded them in the ocean, darting away from even Mayla's keen eyesight. Of all the ways to die, he'd never imagined finding himself stranded on an island without food or water and slowly succumbing to hunger and thirst. Rather, he'd envisioned a glorious death filled with battle, triumph, and pride before entering the doors of Valhalla.

Why hadn't he listened to his mother? He'd thought himself wise at the time but now he realized he was a fool.

Crack!

The sound startled him, and he glanced over his shoulder to find Mayla wrestling open several clams she must have found in the sea. She gestured for him to join him, and together, they consumed what little raw meat lay inside. It wasn't enough to fill their bellies, but it would satisfy their hunger for a short while.

He bit his lip as his attention turned to the seals lingering on the beach, heads upturned as if trying to catch the faintest rays of sunlight breaking through thick clouds. A flash of lightning lit up gray skies, followed by a rumble of thunder. He prayed to Freyr for the dozenth time, begging for the storm to move their way.

"Can I hunt one of your friends to use their meat for food?" Klaus called to Mayla. "Maybe even use the pelt, too."

Her head shot up, her eyes widening in horror at the suggestion. "I will never speak to you again if you do such a thing."

He sighed, trudging his weary feet through the sand, pointing to a random seal. "It's your lucky day, Hilda. You get to live to see another sunrise."

The seal barked as if she knew he was speaking to her. The shadow from a cloud passed over her, and the creature moved to another spot of sunlight. A second seal barked behind him, and he braced himself should it tackle him. But then his brows furrowed together when he realized it wasn't a bark at all, but wood hitting rocks.

He turned toward the sound.

And froze with his feet submerged in the grainy sand. Icy shock jumped up his body and squeezed his chest. The sea buffeted *his boat* against a pair of boulders, the wood battered and worn with the mast and a part of the sternpost broken off, but it was otherwise intact.

"Blades and blood!" he exclaimed loud enough to startle several seals into jumping into the sea. He kicked up sand as he stumbled toward the *skuldelev* and caught onto the prow with as much strength as he possessed, as if the ocean might reach out and try to snatch it from him. "Gefion's luck! I can't believe my eyes!"

Yet, as he ran his hand down the hull of his boat, the rough wood met his flesh, a real, tangible object against his palm. The oar still lay on the shore. And with the boat…

Heart racing, he dragged it through the water, closer to where Mayla watched him from the boulder with a hard, distrustful expression. The fire that had blazed strong in her eyes when they'd first met billowed once more. Raging. All consuming.

"It will get us to where we need to go," he said excitedly.

"Which is where?" she scoffed, turning her face away from him as she crossed her arms.

The water sloshed with each of his steps, soaking his trousers and spraying into his face. His gaze softened as he looked at her, taking in her long, gorgeous hair, the selkie spots on her skin, the adorable pout to her lips. He knew what he wanted. Although he didn't know how to get it, by Thor's hammer, he sure was going to try. "Back home."

Slowly, her arms fell to her sides, and she turned to reveal her surprised yet dubious expression. "What about Lise?"

True sorrow pulled on his mouth until he frowned. Instead of meeting her gaze, he focused on dragging the boat out of the water, grunting with the immense effort it took to flip it over onto the sand to allow the inside to dry. He immediately got to work with repairing the hole with what little supplies he had on the island. "To get Lise back, I would either have to send good men to their deaths by attacking Oswald's clan, or I would have to force your hand, Mayla. I can do neither. Not anymore. The marriage contract is void. Oswald can have his bride. With a witch in our path, there is nothing to be done."

"But…what about the feud? What about your marriage? You are—were—promised to her. You wanted to take her as your bride."

After filling the hole the best he could, he flopped onto the sand, exhausted, using his arm to block out the remaining rays of sunlight from his eyes. "Is being forced into marriage to protect your family deemed as 'want?'" he asked. "I despise Sten Borgen. He killed my fadir. And I'm supposed to be content with taking his daughter as my wife?" He turned onto his side, finally meeting Mayla's brown-eyed stare. "It is not well. And I don't want to pretend it is." With a gentle touch, he skimmed his finger over her bare foot and held her gaze. "There is someone else I want at my side. But how am I supposed to convince her she wants me, too?"

All too suddenly, her foot withdrew beneath her sark. "Your pride will not allow for your retreat."

Shame burned in his chest at the thought of returning to his clan without Lise. Failure to do as he'd promised would be terribly humiliating and might incite further bloodshed. It would also question his position as chief. Someone might use the opportunity to duel him to take his place as chieftain. He also risked waking with a knife in his back to rid of him completely.

However, someone was already out for his blood. No matter what action he took, it would be dangerous for him to return either way.

"I will deal with the consequences," he answered finally.

A raindrop plopped onto his forehead, and then his cheek. He gasped and snapped his attention toward the skies. The dark clouds hovered over them, steadily releasing rain from its depths. In a desperate attempt to drink, he opened his mouth and caught a drop. Even when another drop hit his tongue, despair opened its jaws and trapped him in its maw. It wasn't enough. He could lie in the same spot for hours and it still wouldn't be enough.

Silver light flashed beside him, and he inhaled sharply to find Mayla with her arms outstretched, concentration on her brow. The light of her magic moved between her fingers as if she were weaving a loom.

Little by little, she pulled her hands farther apart as the movement of the light increased. Only then did he notice her intentions.

She was catching the raindrops with her magic and coaxing them toward a curved chunk of inner tree bark, which drained into an empty clam shell. Slowly, water filled the shell, and when it was full, she nudged the piece of bark with her knee so it pivoted enough to start filling another shell.

There were six total shells.

"Unless you want to search for more vessels," she murmured, eyes focused, "I suggest you start drinking."

Like a dying man desperate for the faintest taste of water, he scrambled toward the shells and lifted the first to his lips. The cool water rushed down his dry throat, soothing the scratchiness with each swallow. He consumed the water from each shell before Mayla filled them again. It wasn't much and wouldn't last long, but they now had a boat. It wouldn't need to last too much longer.

Mayla's magic flickered out. As the rain beat upon them harder, they held each other's gaze. A thousand questions floated between them, a thousand words he wanted to say.

But all he managed to ask was, "Why?"

"Because," she murmured, "you have surprised me by how gentle and kind you can be. How dedicated. How loyal. You amuse me. You warm me in my grief and cool me in my rage. I will not allow you to belong to anyone else." She released a shaky breath. "Because you are mine."

"Because you are mine."

Mayla's entire body trembled with her declaration for the human. For the man she had staked a claim on as her mate. For so long, she'd never understood why Erianna had chosen a human for her mate. But now she did. It was easy. To enjoy their presence. Their company. Their humor and their wit.

It was easy to love them.

Despite their rocky beginning and against her better judgement, it was easy to love Klaus.

But as she met his wide-eyed stare, her hands trembled, and her insides quivered. His lips parted but no sound escaped. He stood, and her heart pounded with each step he took toward her. Worry darted through her veins. What was he thinking? Had she been too forward? Too honest? Had she put herself on a fragile, crumbling cliff, only to end up falling onto sharp rocks below? Or—

Her thoughts froze, completely silent as he gently cupped her chin with one large, strong hand and tipped her head so she gazed directly into the blue of his eyes. Blue like a calm sea after a storm. Blue like the skies moments before stars twinkled into existence. Blue like—

He captured her lips with his own, and she inhaled sharply as if the cliff crumbled beneath her feet. But instead of hitting the rocks, she sprouted wings and soared.

Her heart pounded a joyous drum, beating in sync with the rhythm of Klaus's soul. Their souls danced and intertwined in a way she had no idea was possible, and she allowed the rhythm to carry her on a breath of wind.

Slowly, she touched his chest with hesitant fingers, but then more daringly smoothed her hand over his muscles, to his shoulders, and then wrapped her arms around his neck, pulling him closer. His grip tightened around her waist as he deepened the kiss, and she all-too-eagerly responded by returning his affection. She had never kissed a human before, but it was better than she knew was possible.

Although she had only known Klaus for a few days, it felt as if their souls had been waiting for each other for a long time. As if she had lived her entire life waiting to breathe him in.

Her fingers tangled in his damp hair, threading through thick brown locks. Her tongue explored his mouth, meeting each curious touch with a passionate fervor. Her heart burst into flames when he bit her bottom lip, unearthing a playful growl from her throat.

She wanted more. So much more. To make him hers completely, a joining of their bodies, hearts, and souls.

Klaus hiked her skirt up to her thighs, his strong hands cupping the back of her knees. She took advantage by wrapping her legs around his waist. Strong. Sturdy. Handsome. A more than capable mate to protect her and their home and give her pups.

She shook her head, trying to clear some of the foggy steam invading her thoughts, but a rumble of thunder in the sky broke their passionate embrace. Rain fell from the darkened skies in thick sheets, threatening to soak them.

A squeal of laughter escaped her mouth as he picked her up into his arms and sprinted toward the tree line, closer to where he'd built the shelter. A large, unburdened smile spread across his face when he finally set her down beneath a leafy tree, which barely managed to keep the rain from soaking them further.

"The reason I built the shelter was to *avoid* the influence of the elements!" he shouted over the downpour.

"Then I suppose we better make good use of it." She cast him a coy look and then stood on her toes to place a suggestive kiss on his neck before whispering in his ear. "And leave our clothes somewhere they can dry."

His eyebrows lifted in surprise, but then his grin widened as he grabbed her by the waist and pulled her flush against him until the only space that remained between them was a breath between their lips. But he teased her, making her sigh as he kissed her cheek, her jaw, and then her ear.

"On one condition," he murmured.

Confusion joined the frenzy in her heart when, instead of sealing their declarations with a kiss, he stooped down and plucked a piece of grass out of the ground. He lifted her left hand, and only then did her breath hitch when he tied the grass onto her ring finger. The small green blade felt heavy, full of intent.

"Klaus," she breathed. Among selkies, males would present a pearl necklace with the most beautiful variety of colors to tempt a female to become their mate. She'd observed humans long enough to know they often did it with rings. Sometimes with flowers.

"This is my condition." He kissed her finger, and her heart responded with a fluttering weightlessness. "Say you will marry me."

A part of her whispered that she shouldn't do this. That she shouldn't agree. But another part of her shouted louder, drowning out the whisper. They hadn't known each other long, but she was incredibly fond of him, and their souls sang for each other. Surely, the rest of their obstacles would find a way to work out on their own.

"What about—"

"What about nothing," he interrupted in a breathy voice. "I am unattached, and I want you as my bride."

"But how—"

The words disappeared from her tongue, replaced by laughter when he scooped her up once more and ducked inside their shelter, placing her gently on the bed of leaves.

Her gaze softened as she stared up at him, admiring the deep set of intention on his brows and the playful mirth in his eyes.

He traced her skin from her neck to her collarbones, and she sighed against his touch. "Don't make me find creative ways to make you agree to my offer."

Her heart almost thundered louder than the pouring rain pelting the bark shingles above. She could say no. She knew she could, and he would respect her decision. But she didn't want to.

"You are what I want," she whispered, touching his hair, his face, his chest. "I will be your bride. And you will be my mate."

He cast her a devilishly handsome grin and leaned closer until his words caressed her skin. "There is nothing I want more."

And then their lips crashed together again, nothing held back, as their souls joined as one, with the rain as their song and the thunder as their symphony.

CHAPTER 9

Two days. No food. No water. Little sleep.

Anders struggled feebly against the ropes binding him to the brown wooden fence beneath an unforgiving sun. His eyes burned nearly as much as his sunbaked bare back. He wet his dry lips, wincing at the small cracks residing there. His chafed wrists ached from rubbing the rope back and forth, back and forth across the post. Several threads had snapped. Only a couple more to go.

As he attempted to break the remaining rope, he held back a cry of pain. His wrists could not take any more. But he had to keep trying. For his mother. For his sisters. For his clan.

A door slammed from outside the longhouse where the enemy held his family captive, followed by footsteps approaching from the side. Anders positioned his body to hide his progress with the ropes, glaring through aching eyes at the man who had taken so much from him already.

His brothers.

His father.

By Odin's teeth, he refused to allow him to take anything else he held dear.

Sten stopped directly in front of him, and Anders craned his neck to meet his eye. He lowered his voice threateningly. "If I find out you've hurt my family in any way, I will kill you."

"They are fine. For now."

"You are playing a dangerous game, Sten. Do you think my clan will stand for this? They will never bow to you." The other clan members were being held hostage as well. An eerie green magic clung to the doors of their longhouses, keeping them confined and unable to escape. Oswald was behind this. Which meant Sten and his family were as well.

But did that mean…Lise? Klaus's former betrothed? Was she involved, too?

The man stooped until they were eye to eye. "Am I going to have to start killing people to make you comply? Or will I starve them out first?"

"My modir will never become a slave again." He spat at the man's feet. Sten promptly kicked dirt into his eyes. He hissed but otherwise tried to remain stoic despite the agitated tears running down his face.

"I am losing my patience." Sten kicked the bottom of his shoe. "Swear an oath of fealty to me, and *my* clan will follow suit."

"And then what? You will kill my family." He eyed the sword tied to Sten's belt. If he could just reach it…

"I will allow your modir and systirs to live."

"As *thralls*," he emphasized, fury boiling in the cauldron of his spirit, spitting and bubbling over the side of the vessel.

Sten grinned. "Yes, perhaps."

The cauldron within him tipped over, spilling his fury in a mass of liquid-hot water at their feet. He released a war cry, and in his anger, he managed to snap the remaining threads of the rope that bound him. Sten's eyes widened, but he didn't react fast enough before Anders tackled him and punched him in the jaw again and again. He tugged the sword out of the sheath from Sten's belt, and the man barely managed to flinch before he impaled him with his own weapon.

Anders breathed heavily, eyes hard, as the life drained from Sten, followed by the witch's green light flickering out and disappearing entirely along the doors to the longhouses. Although Sten wasn't the witch, he wondered if her power was linked to him in some way.

War cries shook the land as his people flooded out of their houses and met Sten's men weapon to weapon. Anders stumbled toward the family longhouse, using the sword to dispatch two men before he burst inside.

His mother gasped from where she sat comforting his sisters beneath her arm like a mother hen, but then she started to weep at the sight of him. Whether from relief or because he was a ghastly sight, he didn't know.

"Did he hurt any of you?"

They shook their heads.

"Good." He raced into the longhouse and rummaged through his belongings, dressing himself in armor and adorning his weapons.

"Where are you going?" His mother grabbed onto his wrist, stopping him from snatching another knife hidden beneath his bed.

"To find Klaus."

She stared at him, eyes becoming glassy. But finally, she dropped her hand and nodded. "Bring him back."

"I will." *If he is still alive.*

Before uttering another word, he rushed outside, only to find a trail of enemy bodies and the triumphant smiles of his clan members. He glanced between each warrior with no one to lead them in Klaus's absence. No one but…

Me.

Anxiety tumbled in his stomach. Would they listen to him? Could he lead them, even when their rightful leader was gone? He had never measured up to Klaus. His strength. His bravery. His quick thinking. He knew how to command a room, just like their father had.

His legs quivered as he grabbed a shield, stepped up on the same fence post he'd been tied to minutes earlier, and banged his weapon against it. All eyes turned toward him.

"Our clan has been wronged," Anders called out uneasily, a quaver in his tone. But he tried to muster more courage and continued. "We were betrayed. Vows have been broken. Our chieftain is headed toward a certain death." He swallowed, his legs wanting to collapse beneath the ache of several days of sitting in the same position and from not getting enough food and water in his body. "We need—" He stopped and tried to imitate Klaus's steady voice, the voice people always listened to. "We *will* board our boats, find our chieftain, and go viking."

Cheers lifted into the skies, his clan thirsty for blood. And within the hour, they pushed their viking ships into the water, his with a dragon's head, and sailed from one defeated enemy and toward one much stronger.

"What if our chieftain drowned?" one of his clansmen asked behind him.

Anders kept his gaze steady on the horizon, eyes searching for what he hoped wasn't lost to him. "My brodir is resourceful." He believed it. He had to. "He's still alive. I can feel it." *And he might have had help from the selkie.*

If he didn't find his brother, Oswald's clan would soon feel his rage at the end of his blade.

CHAPTER 10

Mayla hardly dared to breathe.

She watched Klaus's chest rise up and down with each slow breath. His normally serious features were relaxed, peaceful in his slumber. A strand of brown hair rested over his eye, and she longed to swipe it out of his face if only to give her another excuse to touch him, to explore every part of him she had not yet explored.

My betrothed. Giddiness fluttered her heart at the word. *My mate.*

The grass tied around her finger caught her attention, and she held up her hand to admire the humble declaration of Klaus's intentions toward her. Although he had not said the words, she wondered if he loved her, even just to some small degree. Selkies often loved fast but fleeting unless they chose someone as their permanent mate. Then their love lasted forever.

But what if he doesn't return my love?

Doubt crept into her thoughts, creating an anxious pit in her stomach.

She lifted her hand with the intention to shake him awake and ask the questions plaguing her mind but paused when she spotted the smallest sliver of iron peeking out from beneath Klaus's discarded shirt.

Her heart squeezed, blood pulsing through her ears as she quietly brushed the clothing aside to reveal a familiar silver ring.

And an iron key…

For a moment, her heart ceased beating as ice crawled through her chest. But then the ice shattered, her blood pulsing faster, hotter, and with sickening dread, especially as she wondered how she hadn't noticed the key during their passionate encounter. Had he hidden it from her? Stashed it beneath his clothing? After all the playful interactions, the flirting, the burning emotions, she'd nearly forgotten the past several days.

Most especially, his betrayal.

She knew exactly what the key unlocked.

Careful not to allow the metals to clack together, Mayla picked up the corded necklace and ran a thumb over the coarse metal key. Some of the metal had rusted, yet the object felt sturdy in her hand. She could almost feel the connection to her seal skin, hiding within whatever containment Klaus had placed it in.

She squeezed her eyes shut and forced herself to take several deep breaths while simultaneously listening to how each of Klaus's slumbering breaths complimented hers. Had he ensnared her with trickery? To make her forget what he'd done so he could force her into a marriage and trap her on land?

She shook her head, chuckling with how silly it sounded. Of course, he wouldn't. After spending the last few days together, she knew he had a good heart. He was honest. Loyal. Dedicated. Kind. And she trusted him.

Then why did she slip the necklace over her head?

She wasn't entirely sure.

"Klaus," she murmured, trailing her hand over his chest to try to wake him. A flicker of a smile appeared on his mouth as he captured her hand and held it against his heart. But his breaths deepened again as sleep pulled him back under.

Once again, uncertainty and doubt pulsed through her body.

Needing some time to herself to sift through her confusion, she slipped her hand out from beneath his, pulled on her clothes, and ducked out of their shelter to meet a sky with the sun breaking through gray clouds.

The fresh air after a storm filled her lungs, clearing her head as she walked along the beach. Sand squished between her toes, a welcome and familiar sensation. Rocks and shells in her path threatened to trip her, but she held each side of her skirt in either hand and stepped carefully. Satisfaction filled her when she realized she was getting better at commanding this body. Although the bottoms of her feet still ached with blisters, the pain wasn't too terrible.

The seals from earlier still lingered on the beach, the lazy creatures forcing her to weave around them rather than move for her. Still, they brought a smile to her face. They were home. Always. No matter where she went or how far she traveled.

"Mayla," a voice said behind her, and she jumped at hearing her name in the selkie tongue.

She spun around, only to face Aislee, who had shed her seal skin and now stood on the beach with only her light brown hair to cover her top half.

Her heart jumped into a frenzy, and instinctively, she glanced back the way she'd come, but Klaus was nowhere in sight. "You shouldn't be here," she said, taking her by the elbow and steering her farther away. "I told you not to return."

"You are my sister. My only remaining blood relative. Of course, I had to return."

Mayla stopped short when she realized it didn't matter. Klaus wouldn't hurt Aislee, nor would he take her seal skin. Wherever she'd left it.

She scanned the beach from her position beneath a tree and found Aislee's skin hidden amongst several other seals. It was safe. At least her younger sister was practicing caution.

"Come home with me," Aislee said, turning her attention back to her. "We will gather the support from our males to take back your skin, and perhaps that will convince you to take one of our own as your mate rather than that..." She grimaced. "...that *human*."

Absently, Mayla stroked the key hanging around her neck. She longed for the freedom of the ocean, of exploration, of home. But... "Klaus will tell me where my seal skin is. He will return it and give me my freedom."

"Will he?" She raised a skeptical eyebrow. "Did he say as much?"

"Well...no. But he will."

Aislee took her by the shoulders and gently shook her. "The story *never* changes! Human steals a selkie skin. He or she hides it to keep their selkie prize. Humans are too afraid to give them back, scared that if they do, their selkie might flee to the ocean and never return."

Mayla felt her chin tremble, and she lowered her gaze to the sand when she realized the truth of her sister's words. Never in her life had she heard a tale of a human and a selkie that ended happily. "But Klaus is…"

"Different?" Aislee shook her again. "If he were different, he would have already told you where your skin is. He would have *trusted* you with the information. He wouldn't hide it *from* you, but guard it *for* you. Fear can never be the base of any relationship."

Please, no. Please, no. Please, no.

"Don't do this," she whispered, already feeling her heart start to crack at the terrible realization—Klaus would have given her freedom back if he truly loved her.

A tear slipped down her cheek.

"It's better to hear the truth from me than to learn it when a child is on the way." Aislee's expression fell into sympathy, her gaze dropping to her belly. "If it isn't already too late." Her sister's voice softened, and she tucked a strand of hair behind Mayla's ear. "Don't make the same mistake Erianna did. Come home with me."

A tear escaped her eye, followed by another. They dripped one by one onto the sand, and as she longingly glanced toward the shelter housing Klaus, her heart cracked a little more. "He will," she tried again, but her voice no longer stood on solid rock but crumbling sand. "I'll go ask him myself. He will tell me the truth."

Her thumb caressed the grass tied around her finger. A promise.

"Mayla." Aislee sniffed, eyes red rimmed and expression filled with devastation. "Erianna is dead. Please don't leave me, too. That man is a human. He will only bring you grief and pain."

With those words, the sandy cliff of her hope crumbled beneath her feet. This time, she didn't soar but landed on rocks sharp enough to pierce her heart. Her words she'd spoken earlier came to mind. *"No selkie would ever sacrifice their seal form. Nothing is worth that."*

Was Klaus?

She bit her lip and turned her gaze toward the sea. Her home. The one place she loved more than anything. She loved her selkie life full of independence, fun, and most especially her sister. The only one still alive. She loved her skin, her magic, and her freedom to roam the waters at her leisure.

She could not live without those things. But what about Klaus?

She lowered her head, her chin trembling. He was a human. He could not be part of that life. And she knew in her heart her sister was probably right. As a human, he would never trust her with the location of her seal skin. He would strip her of her freedom. Forever.

As if sensing her defeat, Aislee pulled her by the hand. "I saw the boat earlier. You will have to take it, as I cannot carry you the entire way."

"I can't leave him here alone," she said miserably. "Stranded. He can't collect water on his own."

"Norse ships left the port last I saw. Perhaps they will come this way. He will be all right." Aislee tugged harder. "We must leave immediately. The sooner we can retrieve your skin, the better."

Klaus patted the space beside him but found nothing but grass and leaves where Mayla had slept. A sense of foreboding gripped his throat, but it loosened its fingers as he forced himself to take a deep breath. Despite his attempt at control, he bolted upright into a sitting position. Something didn't feel right, as if the very air sparked with uneasiness and disquiet.

"Mayla?" But no reply came.

Unfounded panic struck him through the chest as he hastened to pull his clothes on. A thousand possibilities ran through his mind. A shark had eaten her. She got hit by lightning. Or perhaps she was wandering the island alone and happened upon some terrible creature.

He inhaled slowly and released the breath. Of course, she was fine. They were the only ones on the island, after all.

Yet, the foreboding and dread remained, similar to what he had felt only minutes before Oswald had stolen Lise from him. Something was amiss. But he didn't know what.

He bounded across the earth, jumping over protruding roots and ducking beneath a branch. And then he came to a halt at the edge of the tree line, breathing heavily as he spotted his beautiful selkie on the beach.

However, his gut tightened again.

It looked as if another person stood near her, but from this distance, he couldn't truly tell. And when he blinked, he only saw Mayla. And she was pushing his *skuldelev* into the water.

Heart heavy, Mayla and Aislee pushed Klaus's repaired boat into the sea, trying to make as little noise as possible. Water sloshed against the side, loud enough for her to wince. Her gaze darted toward the shelter. The shadows skewed the tree line enough to hinder her sight. But it didn't appear as if Klaus had emerged yet.

"Can you work this vessel?" Aislee asked as she thrust the oar into her hands.

"I-I-I don't know." She stared at the oar, eyes wide. This felt wrong. But what choice did she have? "I will try."

"Good." Her sister stumbled toward her skin, clumsy and uncoordinated but slightly less than her without skirts to tangle in her legs. "I will follow in the water. I'm not comfortable without my pelt."

The hem of Mayla's dress soaked up water as she attempted to hop into the boat but ungracefully swung over the lip and landed in a heap at the bottom of the vessel. She ignored the pain flaring in her shoulder and scrambled for the oar. She barely dipped it into the sea when a hand shot out and grabbed the side of the boat.

Her heart jumped to her throat. Her gaze darted from the hand, up the arm it belonged to, and then her chest squeezed so tight, she felt like it might burst at the seams.

Klaus.

He swallowed, followed by a slow shake of his head.

She couldn't maintain eye contact, especially when the heat of remorse burned her face.

"Please tell me you are scouting out good places to fish," he whispered huskily. She glanced up, only to wince when she found his attention on the key hanging around her neck.

It was enough to implicate her.

She bowed her head, not knowing how to reply. There was no good answer.

When she didn't respond, he spoke again. "Did you take advantage of me? Deceive me?" His voice cracked with emotion. "You laid with me to get the key?"

"No, I swear. That's not why." Yet, as she uttered those words, she still wore the key. "I swear, Klaus. Please believe me."

Again, she looked at him but regretted it. He stared at the sky ahead, blinking rapidly as if barely holding back his emotions. His grip never loosened on the boat. But was he afraid of losing her? Or the way off the island?

"Then answer this question." Blue eyes met her gaze. Begging. Pleading. "What would you choose? Me? Or your freedom?"

She lowered her gaze in shame, eyelashes hiding the guilt in her eyes. Her freedom meant everything to her. She would not give it up willingly. Not even for him.

Wordlessly, he took back his key and pulled the cord over his head, climbing into the boat. He took the oar from her and dipped it into the water, smooth stroke following smooth stroke until they were far enough from the island that she didn't dare jump over the side. Not even when she knew Aislee swam in the water nearby.

"Where are we going?" she whispered, though she already knew the truth. She held her clenched fists in her lap. After everything, he would still take her to Oswald?

A fluid stroke. "I'm finishing what I set out to do. I'm going to Oswald." Pain flashed across his face. "You made your choice."

A wail of anguish and fury stuck fast to her throat. One of her hands moved to cover her eyes and the other to her throat. But the simple touch did nothing to hold back her tears nor her quiet selkie wails. Why did this hurt so much? He shouldn't have so much power to hurt her, but her chest ached as if she were being crushed by a large chunk of ice, followed by blazing heat of fury. Fury at Klaus. At herself.

Klaus swiped at his cheeks but continued rowing. For all his sweet words of promises and dedication, he seemed in a hurry to reach Lise again.

Aislee cut through the water and crashed her body against the small boat. Klaus cursed when he nearly lost his oar, and Mayla held on tight to the sides.

Her sister hit the boat again, followed by a wave of ocean water that washed over the side, drenching Klaus almost from head to toe. He swore again, now fighting for control of the boat, rocking his weight from side to side to counteract the movement of the waves.

Mayla held on, fingers white. Her throat constricted, her breaths coming in rapid spurts. She didn't want to fall in again. The last time had been terrible enough.

"Are you truly trying to drown me?" Klaus's jaw clenched, the pain still lingering in his expression.

Despite her growing fear, she tried to remain stoic. "It's not me. My sister is furious."

"Your sister?" His jaw dropped. "There is another one?" Another string of curses.

The next rock of the boat tipped it so much that Mayla released a strangled cry of alarm, clutching onto the vessel with a death grip. Klaus transferred his weight to the opposite side just in time for it to smash back into the water, sending up a spray of salty seawater.

"Aislee," she growled in the selkie tongue, heart still pounding. "Stop. He is a fragile human."

"He deserves to drown."

"I will never forgive you if you harm him."

Her sister bumped the boat one last time before her head emerged beside them. She spit a stream of water directly into Klaus's face and dove back beneath the surface. He coughed and sputtered, glaring at the spot where the water still rippled from Aislee's departure.

The water calmed. Aislee did not return. Or, at least, she did not show herself or her power again.

"Are there any other sisters I should know about?" But then Klaus shook his head and sighed. "I suppose it does not matter."

She wrung her hands as silence became their lonely companion. Instead, terrorizing thoughts swam in her mind. What would happen when Klaus gave her to Oswald? Would he be cruel? Controlling? Would he hurt her? Was there any way she could convince Klaus not to do this? Oh, but he seemed so angry at her.

A constant ache pounded in her chest. Silent fury boiled her blood. She would not have her freedom. And she would not have Klaus.

She would have nothing of value at all.

Regret soured in her stomach. Far too much regret.

They reached land by the time dusk settled in the sky, but instead of pulling the boat onto the beach, Klaus kept it close to the shore, the oar lying in his lap.

"Get out." His voice was sharp and filled with venom. The look in his eyes cut her to pieces. It was the look of hurt. Of betrayal. "You should be able to reach the bottom."

She did as he demanded, and the water only climbed to her knees. When he didn't follow, she clung to the boat, terrified he might leave without her. Was Oswald waiting for her already? But as she scanned the darkening beach filled with dirt, trees, and rocks, she inhaled sharply when she recognized her surroundings.

They'd returned to Klaus's home.

"Are you not coming with me?" she asked in barely a whisper.

He unstrung the key from his necklace and tossed it toward land. It hit a pair of rocks with a *clang*. He continued to frown. "Follow the beach to the south until you come across an empty, weathered boat. Inside, you will find a chest."

The blood drained from her face when he dipped his oar into the water with the intent to turn back around. She tightened her grip on the boat. "Don't leave like this."

"You wanted your freedom." His throat moved up and down with a swallow. "You have it."

"And what about you?"

"My next actions are none of your concern." He glanced away, but she still caught the sheen of moisture in his eyes. "I apologize for stealing your skin. It was never mine to take."

Her hand fell limp at her side, and he took that moment to row away from her. She watched him go until the moonlight swallowed him whole, heart heavy and eyes brimming with tears. He'd given her a choice. To stay with him on land as his wife. Or to choose the freedom of the ocean.

And she couldn't help but feel the torment that she had chosen wrong.

CHAPTER 11

Mayla walked along the beach with her bare feet, the cold ocean water licking at her toes. Her steps were slow to match the languid beat of her heart. Somewhere deep inside her, she knew if she ever saw Klaus again, he would be married. To someone else. Perhaps even Lise. And it was her doing.

The thought caused her to release an anguished wail. Her mate would be someone else's mate. What a terrible, lonely realization.

Like Klaus had instructed her, she continued her journey until she spotted a small, weathered boat on the sand. Planks of wood had rotted away from the structure, and numerous holes dotted the vessel.

Hope spurred her legs forward, and she bounded toward the boat, feet slapping against wet sand. She stumbled several times on blistered feet but otherwise remained upright. A chest lay inside, and as fast as her shaking hands allowed her, she used the key to unlock it. It swung open to reveal her seal skin, unharmed.

But as she reached for it, she paused.

Was this worth losing the man she loved? Klaus had said he was going to take her home with him. She never gave him the chance to prove to her what his words meant. The first thing he might have done was return this to her, but now she would never know.

She fisted her pelt in her hands and squared her shoulders. She stripped herself of her human garments and in the next moment, the magic of her selkie transformation consumed her, allowing her human form to meld with her selkie form until they were one.

Her seal half felt strong, full of muscle and strength that her other form didn't possess. Although awkward as she lumbered across the sand, the moment she jumped into the refreshingly cold water, the relief of freedom filled her soul. Yet, it wasn't enough. She knew that now. It was nothing without Klaus.

Driven by the thought of him, she darted forward through the water, her eyes seeing clearly beneath the waves. But as she swam, she soon became disoriented, losing sight of the path Klaus might have taken. Her head broke the surface, and she sniffed the very air for his scent. It was faint, hardly discernible, and impossible to follow.

Just as despair started to crush her, a familiar seal swam in her direction.

"He gave it back?" Aislee asked, nudging her with her flippers.

"He did. But now he is gone. I don't know how to find him." A wail of distress escaped her mouth as she darted back and forth, trying to find any sign of him. Her mate. Where was her mate?

Her sister paused to look at her, black eyes watching her carefully. A wave buffeted them, but soon the water calmed. Finally, she spoke, *"Are you sure you want this? The result might only bring heartache."*

"I need him," was her only answer. How could she possibly explain their bearing of hearts and bonding of souls? She refused to allow Aislee to nudge her toward another path. Not again.

Aislee circled her in the water, indecision in the slant of her whiskers, but then she darted in the opposite direction and Mayla quickly followed.

"I don't know which way he traveled after I stopped following to track you," Aislee said, *"but I know where to find humans who likely do."*

Hope built up within her like the fire Klaus had created while they were stranded on the beach together. Warm. Inviting. Beautiful. Maybe she wasn't too late.

The vast blue ocean held an array of creatures from fish to octopus to starfish, most startling awake when they swam past. But then she and Aislee slowed at the sight of the bottoms of large ships sailing through the ocean. Oars dipped into the water in a steady rhythm, propelling them fast and with purpose.

Norse ships.

"These are Klaus's people?" Mayla asked quietly, afraid anything louder might bring attention to them.

Her sister's whiskers twitched. *"I don't know. But they left the port from the land where our sister…"*

Aislee trailed off, and they shared a moment of silence to mourn Erianna. No amount of silence was enough for the dear sister they'd lost. Nothing would ever be enough.

Mayla bobbed her head out of the water and carefully watched the ships. Oars dipped in and out of the sea like the perfectly choreographed dance of dolphin dives. Enormous red and white sails were bloated with the wind like a terrifying beacon of pillaging and destruction. Lanterns hung from posts with wood carved to look like dragon heads. The light illuminated men and some women with black paint in various designs across each face. They appeared fierce, and with weapons strapped to them, they seemed ready for battle.

She moved closer to get a better look at each face. During her short time in Klaus's village, she'd only seen three faces. His, his mother's, and—

Anders!

The brother stood at the front of one of the ships, hand holding the rigging to keep himself steady while he stared forward with a serious expression on his face. The man did not appear similar at all to the jesting person she'd met in the barn.

Here's to hoping they won't skewer me with their spears, she said silently to herself as she bounded toward the ship. Oars narrowly missed her as she tried to swim closer, not bothering to hide herself from their view. Some of the men pointed to her in the water. A couple of them grabbed their spears with the intent to attack.

She jumped out of the water and dived back in, finally getting Anders's attention. He leaned over the side, eyes furrowed as he stared at her. She stared back. In this form, she could not speak to him as she could her sister.

"Halt!" he shouted, and all at once, each person stopped rowing. The sea became eerily silent as everyone aboard now watched their skipper. The few other ships stopped as well. Anders's eyes shot open wide. "The stars!"

Relief rushed through her, and she tried but failed to climb the side of the boat, falling back into the water. Anders, with the help of two other extremely confused men, helped her inside the boat where she landed with a rather ungraceful thud.

"Somebody, hand me a blanket!" Anders shouted, and a man quickly stepped forward with one in tow. Anders held it out, blocking her from view of the other men and averted his gaze to the dark waters.

A shiver of magic ran through her until her two forms split and her seal skin lay in her arms as she shifted back into her weaker human form. She swayed on unsteady feet but otherwise remained standing with a hand braced against the sternpost. She set her skin down, took the offered blanket, and wrapped it around herself, now knowing humans were uncomfortable with her nakedness. Murmurs of astonishment filled the ship as she turned around.

"It's a selkie!"

"Thor's mercy."

"A good omen."

"A bad omen, fool."

"Praise to the gods."

"Who are you?"

She held up her hand to display the grass tied onto her finger. It wasn't made of metal, nor of wood, but it still held a promise. One she wholeheartedly planned to keep. "I am Mayla Brior, betrothed to Chieftain Klaus Lovik." At least, he hadn't ended the engagement, whether from forgetfulness or heartache, she wasn't sure.

More murmurs. Anders's jaw dropped. "How? What? When? It's impossible. You have known each other for a short time. Especially considering how you two left…"

What he didn't mention was she'd been Klaus's prisoner. "Things changed. It does not feel like a short time since we met."

Anders pinched the bridge of his nose. "I suppose marriages have been born from much less. Where is my brodir?" He swallowed. "Is he…dead?"

All eyes watched her carefully for her reaction, as if each wanted news of their chieftain. "He is alive. But I believe he's going to confront Oswald. I don't know how to find my way there."

The man's face fell into a serious mask once again as he shouted orders to the other boats, words she didn't quite understand. Within moments, the ships began to move forward again, but this time in a slightly different direction.

"He's going by himself?" he asked after several minutes. She nodded. "That brave fool." He glanced sideways at her, curiosity in his eyes. "Two women promised to him in a matter of days?" His fingers stroked the short facial hair on his chin. "Either Klaus is really mucking things up, or he possesses more charisma than I thought." A grimace. "I'd rather go with the latter. My brodir has a thick head."

"I won't refute your statement."

Anders laughed, shaking his head. "This marriage should be interesting. I would like to see how it plays out."

Mayla's mouth twitched, but she otherwise kept her gaze fixed on the waters, searching for a much smaller boat that carried the man who held her affection. She didn't find one. "Why were you out here if not to sail to Oswald's home?"

"Klaus is my brodir." He tightened his grip on a rope. "And our chieftain. We were searching for him with a small hope that we might still find him alive."

Shock shimmied down her spine, and she nervously ran her hair through her fingers when she realized it might still end up being the case if they didn't reach him fast enough. "Did you know what happened to his boat?"

"Yes. And we know who did it, too."

A woman approached and set a pile of clothing and furs at her feet, briefly dipping her head in greeting. "I can't imagine you want to be walking around with only a blanket to cover you."

Mayla grimaced as she eyed the clothing. "I would rather not wear human clothes at all."

Both Anders and the woman shared an amused look, and Anders spoke. "It's best you do. And then I will tell you everything I know."

Again, she stared at the foreign objects lying at her feet, the fur tickling the tips of her toes. "I don't know how to put it on. Last time, Klaus dressed me."

Anders pressed a fist to his mouth as if trying to suppress a laugh. "And I'm sure he did a thorough job of it."

Before she could ask after his meaning, he said, "My friend, Anja, will help you." He stared forward. "Oswald will cower before us when we attack the enemy with a selkie at our helm."

"Two," she corrected as she searched the water and spotted Aislee following close to the boat. "If my sister is willing to join your cause."

The man grasped her forearm with a strong grip. "We'd be honored."

CHAPTER 12

The patch in Klaus's boat wasn't perfect.

Water seeped into the vessel, though much slower than before. It first barely dampened the wood. Now it lapped at his shoes. But it didn't matter. Without Mayla to slow him down by a battle of wills and repeated attempts to drown him, he would arrive at his destination just before dawn.

A Mayla-sized hole widened in his heart with her absence. The song it used to sing was now choppy, melancholy, and without rhythm. She had been the beat he danced to. Her very existence was the harmony to his soul.

But she didn't want him.

She wanted the ocean.

And he feared she had never wanted him at all.

Thoughts of self-doubt and the agony of longing plagued him for the entire journey from the northern part of his home until he spotted Oswald's village. It was farther inland than his own, with the most important people housed within the *trelleborg*, a ringed fortress protecting several longhouses, the chief's personal farms, and the meeting hall. Most of the villagers lived outside the fortress, tending to their own animals, farms, and families.

Klaus thanked the semi-darkness of pre-dawn for shrouding him from watchful eyes as he silently cut through the water, mindful of keeping the oar from making a splash. He held his breath, afraid even the slightest noise might alert someone to his presence.

He shook his head, disappointed with himself. He was entering his rival's homeland alone, without a weapon, and with a heart full of sorrow rather than one filled with vigor. It was a venomous recipe for death.

Before the *skuldelev* could scrape across the rocks, he jumped out, quietly submerging his legs up to his knees and slowly guiding the boat toward land. Although he likely couldn't use it again without dumping the amassed water out first, he still hid it between two boulders and prayed no one would come across it on the beach.

Several lookouts passed on the small cliff overhead, and he hid behind a tree, pulse racing, until the light from their lanterns moved out of sight.

This was not how he'd envisioned this happening. He'd originally thought he'd have a selkie by his side, wiping out his enemies with one powerful swoop of magic or intriguing Oswald enough to trade her for Lise.

But now he was a fool with nothing.

If he managed to defeat Oswald in the *holmgang* and bring Lise back home, then what? Could he truly still marry her when his heart sang for another? When the grief over love lost plagued him?

Love...

When two hearts sang the same song, it quickly turned to love. Or so his mother had said. But what if only one heart sang and the other pretended?

He pushed confusing thoughts of Mayla out of his head and continued forward, traveling up a dirt path and through a field of barley. He crouched low as he approached the village, sneaking closer toward the *trelleborg*.

A demoralized breath escaped him. The *trelleborg* stretched high above him with slick logs stacked side by side. To reach the top, he'd need a rope or a ladder. Otherwise, he'd need to go through one of the four gateways.

He searched his mind's eye for the memories of the two times he'd been there in the past. Where did Oswald live within the fortress?

A door thudded shut somewhere in the village, and he tensed. Following the noise, a cow lowed, and a rooster released a crow to welcome the start of a new day.

He relaxed. At least until the sound of approaching voices spurred his pulse into a frenzy. He hugged the side of the fortress, trying to wedge himself into the nearest crack. The voices grew louder, coming directly above him. The footsteps stopped, and he thought for sure someone had seen him below. But then they resumed speaking.

"Still no sign of him?"

An unfamiliar voice.

"Today is the seventh day. I received word he left days ago."

Klaus's blood iced over.

Oswald.

A feminine laugh cooled his blood even further until nothing remained but ash and snow. "You doubted my plan, Oswald? I told you I would sink his *skuldelev*. And obviously, it must have worked."

Lise.

The scent of betrayal stung his nostrils. That was her voice. There was no mistaking the sing-song lilt and the confidence behind each word spoken.

Lise tried to kill me?

His fingers brushed against the ring hanging from the cord around his neck. The very ring the woman had placed on his finger with the intention of swearing fealty to him for the rest of their lives.

Fury bubbled up inside him. Slowly at first. But then it climbed through his blood, burning like acid in his throat, and then settled in the clench of his jaw. He knew he should have walked away then, to return to his boat, to find his way back home. But he was hurt and upset and angry, especially after what happened with Mayla, and only red flashed across his mind. He wanted answers.

And tonight, he would get them.

Klaus didn't bother hiding himself as he strode toward one of the gateways. The guard at the entrance stood straighter at the sight of him, hand resting on the ax hanging at his belt and eyes squinted with scrutiny. The man didn't react fast enough when Klaus darted forward, stole the weapon from his person, and smashed the blunt end of it against his temple. The guard crumpled to the ground, unconscious.

Jaw clenched and eyes blazing, Klaus entered the fortress, glancing around at the longhouses, gardens, and then his gaze settled on the three figures standing high above on the inner wall. He recognized the witch, Oswald, and…Lise.

Her eyes widened with recognition before narrowing with disdain. How had he not noticed before? She was clever. He would give her that.

"I should have known you were a filthy liar." Klaus spat on the ground and then held her traitorous gaze. "You played the part of helpless damsel very well. I applaud you."

Beside her, the witch's hands sparked with green light, but with just one gesture from Lise, the light fizzled out.

Oswald grinned. "Good of you to join us. In a timely manner, too."

Together, all three of them descended a wooden staircase, Lise taking the lead. He tightened his grip on the ax, eyeing each of them and assessing his next plan of action. In a fight against Oswald and perhaps even Lise if she attacked him as well, he could possibly win. But the witch…

His palms perspired as he gave them a dark, silent look. There was no positive outcome for him. He was alone. He found himself facing a great warrior, a witch, and a traitorous former betrothed on enemy territory with only a stolen ax as his companion.

He likely would not survive this.

Unhinged by his foolishness, he chuckled at himself. If this was a fight he was not going to win, then he would make them earn the kill.

Men and women poured out of the longhouses, accompanied by guards with weapons drawn. This had never been a fair fight. It was a trap he had foolishly sailed into.

Despite the despair he felt for himself, he was grateful he hadn't brought Mayla and put her in danger. He would never have forgiven himself.

His gaze darted from the witch, to Lise, and then landed on Oswald. "I declared a *holmgang*. Are you so much a coward that you will have your men fight for you?"

A brief flash of annoyance crossed the other man's expression, but it quickly disappeared as he drew the sword resting in the scabbard tied to his belt. An ax against a sword… Another disadvantage. But he would make do.

He and Oswald circled each other on a patch of dirt while surrounding men beat weapons against their shields to create a deafening clamor. Klaus never took his attention off Oswald and the triumphant smirk blazing in his eyes.

"You still want to fight for Lise?" Oswald jabbed. "She wears my ring on her finger, not yours. Not anymore."

"I want nothing to do with that treacherous snake. I fight for my honor alone."

Klaus struck first, ax against sword. The strength behind the blow seemed to take Oswald off guard, as he stumbled backward, giving Klaus the opportunity to strike out with his foot. Bone snapped. Oswald cried out and sank onto one knee. But he rolled out of the way of Klaus's next swing and stabbed upward. Klaus twisted to the side to dodge the attack and swung with his weapon. Metal clashed against metal, adding to the cacophony surrounding them.

Anger fueled Klaus's strength as they traded blows. Oswald pivoted on one foot while the perspiration inspired by pain dripped down his face. Klaus struck again, again, again, until he found an opening to kick the man's bad leg.

Oswald cried out, collapsing to the ground. Klaus's grip tightened on his ax as he started forward.

"That's enough," Lise said, frowning.

He ignored her, raising his weapon above his head, and—

"I said no more!"

A familiar flash of bright green light smashed into him, chaining his wrists together and next his ankles. He crashed face first into the ground, dirt coating his tongue while his ax thudded just out of reach.

He struggled against the glowing green bonds that held him, but they remained firm like steel. No amount of fighting did any good. Rather, the bonds seemed to grow tighter each time he attempted to climb to his feet.

"You witch!" he shouted, head smashed to the ground. He thrashed, but the magic binding his body held firm. He barely budged against his restraints. "I will kill you for this."

"I don't think you are a match for a witch, Klaus." Lise's expression appeared bored, but she spared a look of annoyance for Oswald.

He spat at her feet. "I was talking about you. Why would you do this?"

Lise kicked his ax farther out of reach and crouched by his side, blonde braid hanging over one shoulder and the ends tickling his nose. She unsheathed a knife from her shoe, and he thrashed again when she slowly lowered it to his shoulder. The first slice was quick, deep enough to leave a scar. A grunt of pain stuck fast to his closed mouth.

"That was for one brodir."

The second slice was deeper, and he couldn't help but cry out at the agony ripping across his shoulder. Blood quickly soaked his clothing, and his breathing became shallow gasps.

"That was for two brodirs."

"I killed *one* of your brodirs," he panted, desperate to put distance between them but unable to. "And only because I was trying to protect my fadir."

The iron of her blade flickered beneath the rising sun. "Ah, ja. Brodir number three."

Her knife moved too fast for him to follow before it cut into him. He bellowed at the agony of the final slice, tears trailing down his face. Weakness plagued him. A cold sweat broke out across his brows.

Oswald grinned from his position behind her, now standing with his arm draped over the shoulders of one of his men. But he said nothing, as if allowing her to speak her peace. She ground her boot into his wounds. Tears of pain trailed down his face. Faster. Hotter.

"Did you truly think I would marry you?"

"Not even to end the feud?" he asked through gritted teeth.

"Oh, I will end it. By killing you. Next, your brodir. Your modir. Systirs. My fadir is already taking care of it while you are away. With no one left to feud with…" She shrugged, giving him an unrepentant grin.

Klaus's eyes widened, his lips parting with the shock of her words. "But your fadir—"

"—never wanted an alliance between our two families." She ran the flat end of her knife against his cheek, wetted with his blood. He didn't dare move. "With you gone, my fadir will become the chieftain of your clan. I will become Oswald's bride. And Oswald will become King."

He turned a menacing glare toward Oswald. "Have you no honor?" he spat at him.

Oswald wiped the perspiration from his forehead with a swipe of his arm, a deadly calm brewing in his eyes. "Honor does not win."

Lise kicked him over onto his back, and although he struggled against his bindings, it was no use. The witch was too powerful.

She grabbed him by the bloodied shirt with one hand, lifting the knife with the other. "I will see you in Valhalla."

Battle cries rang in Mayla's ears as Klaus's clan engaged with the enemy upon the beach. Weapon clashed against weapon. A blur of furs, iron, and humans confused her senses. But despite her disorientation, she followed close behind Anders as he fought through enemy after enemy. A powerful wave of water crashed on the land, sweeping their foes off their feet. Aislee had agreed to help them. Though, only because Mayla had begged.

Her heart pounded within her as she searched each face. Where was he? Where was he!

She spotted his boat on the shore, hidden between two boulders, and dread slid down her body and dropped to her toes. Klaus was already here. What if he was dead?

She quickly shook the thought from her mind and continued forward with renewed determination. Magic flowed to her fingertips, the essence of the earth bending to her will. An enemy swung at her with a blade. With a single flick of her wrist, the branches of a nearby tree wrapped around his arm and tugged him backward until he lay sprawled across the sand.

A rush of energy drained from her with the feat, leaving her momentarily winded. She clenched and unclenched her fingers. She could not use her magic again. Not until she found Klaus, lest she lose the battle before it truly began.

Moving closer to Anders, she allowed him to create a path for her, one flecked with blood and battle cries. A second wave of water spilled over the sand, grabbing the enemies' ankles, and pulling them out to sea. They flailed and splashed in their attempt to return to land, but by then, many of them were held at blade-point, forced to surrender.

"With me!" Anders shouted, gesturing for her to follow.

Her entire body protested against moving quickly across loose sand, then slippery rocks, and finally soft grass, but her heart urged her faster. It beat with a desperate hope. *Klaus. Klaus. Klaus.*

The sight of a large, rounded structure stopped her in her tracks, and she stared up at it with wide eyes, a thundering pulse, and lungs heaving with exertion. Large. Thick. Guarded. Impenetrable.

Guards shouted at the sight of them before drawing their weapons and rushing forward. Anders simply grinned and hefted his sword up with both hands. "Get inside the fortress. Find Klaus. If I don't make it—"

"Your brother will never forgive you."

He gave her a curt nod before rushing forward to meet the first guard. Mayla darted in another direction, the path to the fortress free from obstacles when Anders took the brunt of the attention. Her legs ached, feet blistered, but her desperate need to see Klaus safe and whole kept her together.

She rounded the corner of a gateway, out of breath and weighed down by awful, heavy human clothing. Her body swayed with fatigue, and she nearly rested her shoulder against the entrance when she spotted a figure on the ground, bound by magic ropes. A woman with long, blonde hair knelt beside him, a knife poised over him and ready to strike.

Klaus.

"No!" she screeched. Her magic reacted on instinct, reaching into the ground and pulling hard. A mound of earth shot upward and smashed the woman against the trunk of a large tree. She slumped onto the ground, unmoving.

An older woman pivoted on her heel and raised her arms. Green bolts of energy shot from her hands, striking Mayla in the shoulder. Pain crackled down her arm as the force of the blow knocked her off her feet. She hit the ground hard.

"Mayla!" Klaus shouted while frantically trying to escape his bonds. He bucked and thrashed, but to no avail.

A second crackle of energy shot toward her. She rolled out of the way and onto her feet, and it struck the dirt instead.

She and the witch stared at each other, each assessing the other. The older woman was short, gray hair frizzed from her magic. Heavy wrinkles sat on her face, and bony fingers lifted, poised for another wicked spell.

Mayla's gaze darted toward Klaus, to the witch, and back to Klaus. Her stomach turned at the sight of him. Blood soaked his sleeve and one side of his shirt. A paleness consumed his face, likely from losing too much blood.

Slowly, she moved to stand in front of him, providing protection from the witch and the other men keeping their distance, wary of her power.

"Release my mate from his bonds," she ordered.

Behind her, Klaus inhaled sharply but she kept her gaze fixed on the greatest threat in the vicinity. The witch's eyes narrowed, and her stance widened. A flicker of green sparked between her fingers.

So be it.

Magic burned through her soul, growing hotter and hotter as she allowed its wildness to consume her. Fog crept into the fortress, bounding across the earth like rabid dogs. The wind picked up around them, grabbing at her skirts and her hair. Fatigue slammed into her, but she stretched the roots of her magic through the earth and sucked it dry to sustain her. All around her, trees began withering, grass became dry and brittle, and the moisture in once-fertile ground dried up and hardened.

Her power continued to grow, silver flickering through her fingers, ready to be coaxed into action. The witch shot a green bolt at her, and she barely managed to catch it between her hands. The force of the blow caused her to slide back through the dirt, slippery under her feet. She gritted her teeth, eyes watering, and then with one giant push, she shot the bolt back at the witch.

It missed, striking the fortress above her head instead.

Fire burst to life, rapidly climbing the dry logs. Smoke filled the air, choking, suffocating. And with the distraction of frantic shouts and running humans, Klaus's bonds fell away.

Hope flaring bright within her, she thickened the fog to obscure her as she grabbed onto his hand and helped him to his feet. Green bolts flashed through the haze of smoke and fog, which only managed to spark more fires.

Klaus grabbed her shoulder and pulled her down just as a bolt soared over their heads. And then they started running, hand in hand, away from one chaos and toward the next.

Too quickly, he began to slow when they reached a group of buildings outside the fortress. Fighting continued to rage around them. Acrid smoke filled the skies. Women and children ran in one direction while the men were rounded up as prisoners in another.

"Uh!" Klaus grunted after tripping over a rock, barely catching himself from falling.

Worry shot through her. She tugged on his hand and pulled him behind a barn to allow him to catch his breath from his injury. As well as to recover from the exhaustion of using her magic.

She glanced around the corner of the barn, eyes searching for the witch. Rain sprinkled over her head as the growing fog obscured her view of the surrounding landscape. Where was she? The old woman was still a danger to them all.

"Why have you come back for me?" Klaus gasped between breaths. He leaned his head back against the wood. His expression crumpled with agony. His eyes squeezed shut as if his surroundings spun. Fresh blood continued to soak his shirt. He needed stitches. He needed a healer.

He needed *her*.

"Because I made a mistake." She took his hand and kissed his wrist, and his eyes flew open. Blue eyes were surrounded by a ring of agony but sparked with hope. "My freedom means nothing if you are not in my life."

His lips parted, and for a moment, he said nothing. But then he spoke. "I don't want to strip you of what you love most."

She stepped closer and skimmed a finger from his temple to his chin. "There is something I love more," she whispered huskily, looking back and forth into each of his eyes. "And I can't bear to lose him."

"Mayla, *hjartað mitt*," he whispered, taking her by the chin and pulling her closer until their lips brushed in the sweetest caress. And then he murmured the term of endearment again in her ear for her to understand. "My heart."

Her stomach fluttered pleasantly at his words, and she knew in that moment, she would give up anything for him. Everything.

An explosion of fire shook the earth, turning her adoration into panic. She pulled him down for one more kiss before slipping her fingers through his. "We must get to the ships, and then I can heal you."

But when she attempted to tug him forward, he planted his feet and pulled her back until he stood in front of her. "I may not have a weapon, but you will not be my shield."

Her heart warmed, yet she chuckled humorlessly. "This is the second time you have lost your weapon. Can't keep it on your belt, can you?"

His mouth twitched at her jest as he led her through the dense smoke, keeping her close behind him. "Can't keep a weapon on my belt if someone keeps taking my belt off."

Despite the intense situation, she laughed at his insinuation. "It's not easy, I assure you. Human clothing is confusing."

He grinned as he glanced at her over his shoulder, but then his gaze landed on the grass tied around her finger. He swallowed. "You still have it."

"I mean to keep my promises to you." She squeezed his fingers. "All of them."

Another blast rattled the very air around them, cutting their conversation short. Green sparks lit up the sky like emerald lightning. And as if summoned, the clouds further darkened and released torrents of rain. One of the drops splashed against her cheek in their flight toward the ships. Another hit her nose.

This time, Klaus stumbled, unable to catch himself before his knees hit the dirt. He groaned, and his skin seemed even paler than earlier. She latched onto his elbow and hefted him to his feet.

"You will *not* die from this!" she growled, patting his cheek when he swayed on his feet.

"No." He blinked sluggishly. "But I think I'm going to lose consciousness."

She patted his cheek again, this time harder, and his eyes opened wider. "Look!" With a finger, she pointed to the shore down the steep incline. The ocean sparkled beneath the first rays of morning, bathing the Norse ships in stunning light. Bodies and weapons littered the sand, but many others were corralled in a circle, held as prisoners by Klaus's clan. "We are almost there. You will make it, Klaus. Just a little farther—"

A shriek left her lips when someone grabbed her from behind. A strong arm pressed against her throat and blocked her airway. She elbowed and kicked the person who held her captive, but their hold on her only tightened.

"What have you brought me, Klaus?" Mayla's spine chilled at the icy tone in her ear, but when she struggled again, the arm against her throat tightened. "I've always wanted a selkie at my fingertips."

The man removed his arm from her throat, and she gasped in a breath of air. Only to freeze when he pressed a dagger to her neck instead.

Panic clouded Klaus's eyes, his body rigid. Yet he appeared calm as he raised a cautioning hand. "Oswald…" He swayed on his feet, taking a shuddering breath and blinking slowly. "Let her go. Your fight is with me. She has nothing to do with this."

The mention of the man's name chilled her blood. Her hands trembled and her teeth threatened to chatter. Or was the temperature dropping? Not only did the rain add a chill to the air, but something else created the cold. Something unnatural.

"I will not allow you to keep her." Oswald chuckled as he wrapped an arm around her waist and pulled her against him. "Either she will die as yours, or she will live as mine. That is for you to decide. Bring me her seal skin or I will slit her throat."

"I-I-I don't know where it i-i-is." Klaus's teeth chattered as if he, too, felt unreasonably cold. He swayed again but managed to stay upright. His nostrils flared when Oswald pressed the knife even closer.

Mayla whimpered. She didn't want to die, but she refused to live as this man's thrall.

Frost climbed tall blades of grass, and the temperature cooled further. She glanced to her right to find the witch approaching slowly, spear raised and hands crackling with green energy. The woman was powerful if she had strength enough to exhaust her magic and still have more to spare.

A spark of her own magic pricked her fingers, but she cried out when Oswald pressed the blade into her throat, enough to draw blood. Klaus tensed. She swallowed but regretted the action when another trickle of blood dripped from the small wound.

"Klaus," she whimpered, hair matted with rain and lips now numb from the frost clinging to the very air. "I'm sorry."

CHAPTER 13

She squeezed her eyes shut, refusing to witness Klaus's expression. If this was the only way to save his life and get him help, she would do it. "My skin is in one of the ships. Take me there, and I will retrieve it."

Oswald leaned closer until his mouth nearly brushed her ear. She shuddered. "If you try anything, I will kill you, and then I will kill him." He nodded toward Klaus. "Understand?"

With the knife close to slicing her, she didn't dare speak nor acknowledge him with a nod. He seemed to take her silence as acceptance and guided her down the dirt hill leading toward the beach, each step slow and hesitant, though with a limp as if he'd received a recent injury. The witch herded Klaus behind at spearpoint.

The people of both clans on the shore fell silent as they shuffled toward the ships. Oswald continued to hold the knife to her throat, positioning her between himself and Klaus's clan. All eyes followed them. Anders's expression hardened at the sight of his brother, his knuckles turning white around his ax.

Please don't interfere, she wanted to caution.

All she desired was for Klaus to get help and to leave further unharmed. She didn't know what would happen to her. She suspected she wouldn't like it. But Aislee might be able to help later.

As they neared the sea, Mayla caught sight of Aislee darting back and forth in the water, angry and agitated.

Mayla opened her mouth to warn her off, speaking in her tongue. "Don't try—"

"Stop talking," Oswald growled, moving the knife just enough for another drop of blood to trickle down her collarbone. "Where is the skin?"

With a trembling finger, she pointed to Anders's ship. A moment later, the witch clambered onto the vessel and returned with triumph on her face, the pelt in her arms.

Mayla's heart sank at the sight of it, followed by waves of dread that continued to grow larger and larger until they threatened to consume her.

"Don't do this, Oswald," Klaus slurred, tipping one way, and then the other. "She deserves to be free. Not ruled under your thumb." He swayed again, dropping to one knee.

"I don't care what your blind heart thinks." Oswald kicked sand toward him and dropped his knife from her throat to hold her skin. Watching as he ran his hand from her skin's head to her lower back sickened her.

The man's hard gaze latched onto her. Cold. Unforgiving. "Drown them all."

"Drown?" she breathed, a sour taste in her mouth. She glanced toward Klaus, then Anders, and then his clan and the people they held captive. *Oswald's* people. The people shouted and protested, but Oswald refused to heed them.

But why not order the witch to do it instead?

The witch's eyes were sunken into her wrinkles, her lips pale, and she leaned heavily on one of her legs. Her previously frizzed hair now lay damp and stringy against her cheeks.

With a start, Mayla realized the witch had already reached capacity with her magic. The woman was collecting energy by storing her surroundings' heat within her body, which was likely why everything was frosting over.

"I cannot do that."

He held her skin higher. "Then let us start with something inconsequential and work up from there, shall we?"

In the flash of a movement, Oswald's knife cut off her pelt's whiskers.

"Stop!" she screamed, her eyes widening in horror. She lunged for it but stopped short when he held the knife dangerously close to her pelt's head. It was the situation with Klaus all over again. Except this time, she knew Klaus wouldn't have harmed it. Oswald already had.

"What will we do next?" he asked, eyes colder than the deepest part of the ocean. "You can survive without a few of your teeth."

Oswald dug his knife into her skin's mouth and popped out a tooth. She shrieked, tears streaming down her face. "I beg you to stop. Please. Please!"

"Then drown them."

Klaus's arms shook as he stood on his feet and moved closer to them, but the witch quickly threatened him with her spear. "Oswald, surely she can come to some other arrangement." His words came out choppy, eyes unfocused. "You don't want to drown your own people. And if you harm her skin too much, you will have no leverage over her."

Heartache and devastation stared back at her through his eyes, surely mimicking her own. They were two fish caught in the jaws of a massive shark. It wasn't supposed to happen this way.

In the water, Aislee grew more restless, swimming back and forth faster and faster by the moment.

Instead of listening to Klaus, Oswald grinned and dug the knife in again, popping out a second tooth. Mayla wailed at the mutilation of her pelt, accompanied by her sister's cries of empathy. Tears blurred her vision, but she quickly swiped them away when the ocean water began to recede from the shore. It accumulated slowly and built up height until it reached the tallest tree on the beach.

"Aislee, no!" she tried to shout through the accompanying wind whipping at her hair and the salty droplets stinging her face. However, her words were lost in the deafening roar of the water.

Oswald grinned.

But instead of Aislee drowning the humans on land, she whipped the water toward them and knocked Oswald off his feet, smashing his head against sharp rocks, and dragging him into the ocean.

The witch wasted no time.

Green magic wrapped around the spear in her hands as she pointed it in Mayla's direction. She inhaled sharply but had no time to dodge to the side before the weapon vaulted toward her.

Two hands forcefully shoved her out of the way. She landed roughly on the sand, skirt around her knees and palms stinging from the impact. But as her gaze darted back up, the entire world froze. Her heart stuttered. Her breath faltered in her lungs.

The spear that had been meant for her now protruded from Klaus's chest.

The green light flickered out. He stumbled backward. Her own screams drowned in her ears. She clawed her way toward him. His knees buckled, and she barely caught him beneath the arms before lowering him gently onto the ground.

Her heart caught. Deep, red blood soaked his shirt and dribbled out of the corner of his mouth. His hands shook. His face was pale. He blinked sluggishly. Still alive.

Another scream, a violent scream, erupted from her mouth, and the earth shuddered. A hole in the sand ripped open beneath the witch's feet.

And swallowed her completely, followed by an eerie hush prowling the beach.

Drops of rain falling from the heavens grew louder, heavier, filled with heartache and pain. Chaos surrounded her as Anders and his men jumped into action, but all she managed was to stare down at her beloved mate as he gazed at the sky, eyes unfocused.

"Klaus!" she cried, words strangled in her throat. She cradled either side of his face, shaking him to try to keep him conscious. "Please don't die." She sobbed. "Please don't leave me."

Finally, his gaze found her, and he offered the faintest smile that quickly transitioned into a grimace. He cradled one of her hands with his own, fingers trembling.

"With Odin and the other gods as my witnesses…" Klaus coughed, blood spurting out of his mouth while his grip on her hand became weaker.

"No, no, no!" she whispered, voice hoarse. But he continued.

"I promise…" Another cough. "…to love you, to cherish you…" His chest heaved, hands trembling as he winced. "I give you all that is mine to give. I shall honor you…" His eyelids fluttered closed. "…above all others. I shall love you with the ferocity…of a thousand storms… And so, I bind myself…" His hand went slack, and three final words left his lips. "…to you forever."

Silence.

Rain spattered across his face and diluted the blood running out of the corner of his mouth. It soaked her hair, clothing, and dripped from her chin and onto his chest, mingled with her tears.

"Klaus?" she breathed, staring wide-eyed at his limp, unresponsive body. Horror spread through her, growing, suffocating, consuming. "Klaus!" she wailed. She tightened her grip on his face and shook him. "No, no, no, please no."

She checked his pulse. His heart beat slower…slower…slower…

A man dropped a bag on the sand beside them, one of Anders's men, but as she glanced up to meet his eye, she didn't recognize him, nor the words he said to her.

He spoke slower and pointed to himself. "Barber surgeon." And then he reached into his bag and pulled out strange tools and vials of unfamiliar liquid. The man placed a vial against Klaus's lips, but in a moment of panic, she batted the item away and watched as it skittered across the sand.

She shook her head and tightened her grip on her beloved. "Mine," she whispered, and in her desperation to keep him alive, she released the floodgates of her magic.

Blinding silver light poured out from her, filling the skies, bursting against the ground. Some of it leaked into Klaus while the rest ran wild with no target or direction. Energy drained quickly from her body, her skull pounding and her head spinning.

Frustration escaped her lips as a growl. She immediately stopped her efforts, panting hard at the physical exertion of the hopeless act. "My magic is too wild," she sobbed. "It's spilling everywhere!"

She gazed down at Klaus again, paler than before as the life slowly slipped from him. There had to be a way to save him. There had to be a way to—

Her gaze snapped toward the barber surgeon's bag. He protested but didn't stop her as she reached for it and dumped out all its contents. Desperate fingers sifted through the items and scattered them everywhere. Knives. Herbs. Foreign tools.

Hope sparked, lighting a fire within her as she spotted a mortar and pestle. A vessel. Something to contain her magic!

She snatched the two objects from the pile and held the mortar tightly between both of her hands. Taking a deep breath to calm herself, she exhaled slowly and once again released her magic. But instead of spilling back to the earth, she directed it into the mortar.

Silver light circled her in a frenzy, the wind picking up ferociously around her. Her hair whipped around her face. Her clothing flapped in the fierce gale. Shouts echoed on all sides of her, but no one touched her. She kept her focus on filling the mortar with her healing magic. Yet each second spent was another second wasted. It was taking too long! Trepidation began to set in. Klaus was going to die. Not enough magic filled the mortar to heal him.

It isn't enough. It isn't enough. It isn't enough.

Her frantic gaze darted to his pale face. His chest rose up and down almost imperceptibly. More blood escaped his mouth and ran down his chin. A heavy ache settled within her when she realized she could not live without him. If she did not find a way to save him, she would never be whole again, never complete.

Her fingers fluttered over his chest, hovering but not touching. Blood turned the sand red but instead of inspiring fear, it sparked a memory.

Her breath caught as she remembered the runes Klaus had taught her in the sand. His words rang in her mind.

"My modir used to say there was no magic greater than true love."

Concentrating her magic with every fiber of her being, it began to take a different shape, becoming a blinding light at the bottom of the mortar. Symbols began to appear as her magic etched them into the vessel.

True love.

The runes burned brighter and brighter, almost too glaring to look at. But she never tore her gaze away. Black granite crackled with silver sparkles as her magic infused with it. She gave everything—her heart, her soul, her entire being. She offered every last drop of magic to the vessel, forsaking her seal half in the name of love. She would rather be bereft of magic and the sea than to live one day without Klaus.

Finally, the fierce gale calmed into a gentle breeze, lifting the loose strands of hair around her face. Weakness plagued her body, an uncomfortable vulnerability remaining behind in the absence of her magic. It was gone. All of it. Rather, it bounced and swirled like smoke within the mortar, eager for direction.

Her chin trembled as she glanced from the vessel to Anders, who stood nearby with a grief-stricken expression, and then to Klaus who looked as if he might take his last breath at any moment.

"With Odin and the other gods as my witnesses," she started, repeating Klaus's vows as she ground the magic with the pestle, sealing it within the vessel. "I promise to love you, to cherish you." A tear fell down her cheek. "I give you all that is mine to give. I shall honor you above all others." She carefully poured her magic over Klaus's body. The silver light sank into him rather than bounded away. Her heart trembled with hope. "I shall love you with the ferocity of a thousand storms. And so, I bind myself to you forever."

More silence as if everyone within the vicinity held their breath, praying for something to happen. She clutched onto Klaus's hand, pressing his limp fingers to her mouth. The mortar continued to crackle, infused with her magic. Within sight, but just out of reach. This was her only chance. If this didn't work, there was nothing more she could do.

In a sudden movement, his body pushed the spear out of his chest and onto the sand, and she watched, dumbfounded, as the skin around the wound began to reknit. It started slow at first, closing the gaping hole, and sped up until only a silvery scar remained. The gashes in his shoulder followed, closing the wounds and leaving three scars.

Mayla clung tighter to his hand, hardly daring to breathe. *Please. Please. Please.*

She kissed his fingers, his palm, his wrist. Watching. Waiting. Hoping.

But as the seconds ticked by and he continued to remain still, her hope slowly crumbled until it became ash at her feet. His chest rose. And fell.

It did not rise again.

"Klaus." Her voice quivered, her eyes wide. She shook his head. She gripped his shoulders. She placed her hand over his heart. He couldn't be gone. He just couldn't!

"Barber surgeon," she said, her hands fluttering. "What can—"

Klaus gasped in a breath, eyes wild as he struggled into a sitting position. His breaths came in rapid spurts, gaze frantically jumping around.

A sob of relief escaped her as she cradled his face, forcing him to look at her. "You're all right," she soothed. The tension in her body collapsed, and she sagged against him. She inhaled his comforting scent, finding solace in the warmth of his body seeping into her.

After several moments, his breathing calmed. "Mayla," he murmured into her shoulder, wrapping his arms around her waist.

Shouts of triumph filled the skies, and more than once, Klaus's people patted him on the back. But she simply held him, having no energy to do anything more. Healing him had taken too much from her. But it had been worth it.

When she pulled away just enough to look into his eyes, she said, "I choose you. Between my freedom and you, I will always choose you."

He placed his hand over hers where it rested against his chest. "I don't ever want to take your freedom again. You don't have to choose."

"But I already did." She lovingly stroked his face from his temple to his cheek to his jaw. "My seal half has withered away." A pang hit her chest at the reminder. "It took too much magic to save you."

He squeezed his eyes shut and sighed. "Forgive me. I am so sorry."

"I'm not." She kissed one corner of his mouth and then the other, not caring who witnessed her actions. Judging by the deafening roar of hoots and whistles that followed, likely his whole clan was watching. "I would do it again if it meant your heart beat one more time."

A shuddering breath escaped his lips, and then he turned his head to kiss her palm.

Anders approached, slapping Klaus hard on the shoulder while he wore a giant grin. "I thought you had greeted our fallen kinsmen at the veil of Valhalla."

"I am not yet gone, Brodir."

He continued to grin unrepentantly as he glanced back and forth between them. "You two are married."

"We're...*what?*"

"You spoke vows before the gods. You are sealed together. As husband and wife. It's done."

Mayla held her breath, waiting for Klaus's reaction.

But then a smile slowly spread across his face, and he met her gaze with a sheen of happiness in his eyes. "Is that right? But you have not even given me a ring."

Mischief lay at the corners of his mouth. She rolled her eyes and playfully shoved his shoulder before sifting her fingers through the sand, only to find a limp piece of seaweed.

He raised an eyebrow but said nothing as she took his hand and tied it onto his finger. "Now we are bonded," she murmured.

He laughed, eyes shining bright as he shook his head. "This is the strangest wedding I have ever witnessed. Though…" Another grin. "We are supposed to seal it with a kiss."

"Gladly," she breathed, and she stifled his laughter with her mouth, pulling him into a kiss filled with relief, happiness, and longing. She never thought her life would take a turn like this. But she was glad for it. She looked forward to discovering all the mysteries that shrouded humans.

When another round of shouts and whistles erupted around them, they broke the kiss, each laughing and clinging tightly to the other from where they still sat in the sand. Her body felt so weak that she wasn't sure she could stand even if she tried. Klaus might have to carry her to the ship. Then again, someone might have to carry him, too.

At the reminder that her body was now stripped of magic, she glanced toward the mortar and pestle. But then her heart gave a start.

The mortar and pestle…

They were gone.

CHAPTER 14

Even after the immense happiness Klaus and Mayla had experienced, grief still lay thick in the air. He, his new bride, his family, and Aislee lumbered across the rocky shore toward the grave where Erianna rested.

Mayla's red, puffy eyes stared back at him, and as if needing comfort, she reached for him and intertwined her fingers with his. He only wished he could offer more solace than this.

Aislee held her seal skin tight in her arms, glancing warily at Anders.

"Why do you keep looking at me suspiciously?" he asked, his mouth curving into a grin.

"Mayla told me you wanted her skin for yourself. You will not take mine."

"I never planned to. But..." His eyes sparkled humorously. "Just think about how your sister will be on land.

Makes it tempting to be closer to her, no? Maybe through a marriage?" He wiggled his eyebrows suggestively.

Klaus pushed his brother in the shoulder. "Leave her alone, pig breath. They are trying to grieve, and you are not helping."

Mayla stepped forward, slowly approaching a mound on a hill covered in white flowers fluttering over green grass. He watched as she knelt on the grass, soon joined by Aislee. The two grasped hands and bowed their heads.

His heart caught, and he dipped his chin. He'd prevented Mayla from properly mourning her deceased sister. He also wished she did not have to suffer so.

At the reminder, he glanced down at Mayla's decaying seal pelt in his arms, once full of life and vigor, now limp with death. She had given up so much for him. The sea. Her pelt. Her freedom of the ocean. He felt like he had nothing substantial to give in return.

"What are they saying?" his mother asked beside him, nodding her head toward the two selkies who now chanted in a different language. The sound was beautiful. Haunting. Full of anguish and mourning.

"I don't know," he murmured.

A chill raked down his spine when several brown heads bobbed out of the water to his left, staring at him with intelligent black eyes. Those were not regular seals. They were selkies.

He braced himself for them to come on land, shedding their skins, and skewering him alive like Mayla had said they would days ago. But instead, the selkies released similar cries of anguish until the skies filled with a deep mourning.

Slowly, he approached Mayla and Aislee from behind, still worried one of the other selkies might attack him for getting too close. He felt several pairs of gazes on his back, but no one stopped him as he laid Mayla's seal skin on the ground beside Erianna's grave.

Mayla's voice caught. Her shoulders began shaking. And the moment tears dripped unceasingly from her eyes, he knelt beside her and pulled her into the comfort of his embrace. He swallowed a lump of emotion, his eyes burning with regret. Words refused to escape his mouth, stuck in globs of sticky sorrow. He would give the world for his darling selkie. He only wished she hadn't had to give it to him first.

Vines snaked out of the ground, climbed over the seal skin, and covered it until no spot of brown remained. Dirt fell away as the ground opened, the vines lowering the skin into the earth and covering it back up. Similar to the grave next to it, white wildflowers sprouted out of the ground.

Mayla's shoulders stopped shaking, and she held tightly onto one of his hands, kissing each knuckle as if telling him her sacrifice was worth it.

As he held his wife close, he vowed to give her every happiness. This was not the end, but the start of a beautiful beginning.

The last time Klaus had taken Mayla on a boat, she had been his captive, forced to accompany him against her will. Now, as she sat across from him, sunset colors of orange, yellow, and pink splashing against the surface of the calm sea, she accompanied him of her own free will.

A smile tugged on her lips as she watched him, concentration in his brows, while he rowed the oars. Strong. Confident. Serious. But with an underlying wit she adored.

He lifted his head and met her gaze, his expression falling into momentary surprise before he reflected her smile. "Why are you looking at me like that?"

"Like what?" she asked innocently, running her fingers through her long brown hair.

He nudged her foot with his, a flash of mischief in his eyes. "Like you want me to dress you down right here on the water."

Her eyebrows shot up, followed by a scowl, and he doubled over laughing before scrambling for one of the oars he nearly lost in the process. "I'm jesting, love." He caught her hand and kissed it, never failing to coax heat to her cheeks. With a gentle tug, he pulled her onto his lap, and she held him around the neck, wanting to be as close to her mate as possible. To touch him. To breathe in his scent. To enjoy his very presence.

A sigh escaped her mouth as he pressed his lips to her throat. "I have something for you," he murmured against her skin. "A gift."

Eyelids fluttering closed, she murmured, "By all means, keep going."

"Not that kind of gift," he chuckled, though he placed one more kiss beneath her ear before he leaned away and picked up a leather pouch beneath his seat.

The breath fled from her completely as he pulled out a beautiful strand of pearls with sheens of white, pink, purple, and blue. She brushed a finger over each smooth, round pearl, awe filling her entire being. They were gorgeous, breathtaking. No other object within the sea compared to the merit of a pearl. In a selkie union, it was supposed to symbolize strength, beauty, sacrifice, and oneness with each other.

Klaus rubbed the back of his neck and glanced away. "It wasn't easy finding the pearls, but I admit I had Aislee's help. I hope the meaning of it isn't ruined."

"Not at all," she finally managed to say in a quiet, reverent tone. "I love them, Klaus." She rested her forehead against his. "I love *you*. You give me every happiness."

He helped her clasp the strand around her neck, and she once again admired the pearls. She never planned to take them off.

Not even a second later, his grip tightened on her as he started to stand, rocking the boat with his movement. She clutched onto him, uneasiness filling her as she glanced toward the sparkling water of the ocean.

"As my wife," he grunted as he tried to keep his balance, "you are going to have to learn to swim."

She clung tighter. "What are you doing?"

"Throwing you in. It's how my fadir taught me. Sink or swim, he said."

"Don't. You. Dare." She squirmed against him, trying to free herself from his arms. But all she managed to do was rock the boat and knock him off balance. They both toppled over the side with a resounding splash.

Mayla shrieked as the cold sea rushed over her. She clawed at the water, desperate to keep herself afloat when her wet clothing dragged her down. Water splashed in all directions, dripping from her hair and face. But then strong arms wrapped around her waist and pulled her close.

She clung tightly to Klaus, eyes wide and chest heaving. At least until her heart calmed. She chuckled, and he followed suit. Soon, both were laughing and splashing the other, all while he held her securely in his arms—the only place she ever wanted to be.

Klaus's grip on her changed until he held her tenderly, safe within his embrace. They rested their foreheads together, and she released a contented sigh.

His next words sounded like a vow, a promise of love and devotion her heart couldn't help but accompany with her own song. "My love. My life. *Hjartað mitt.*"

Continue the magical Mortar and Pestle adventure with…

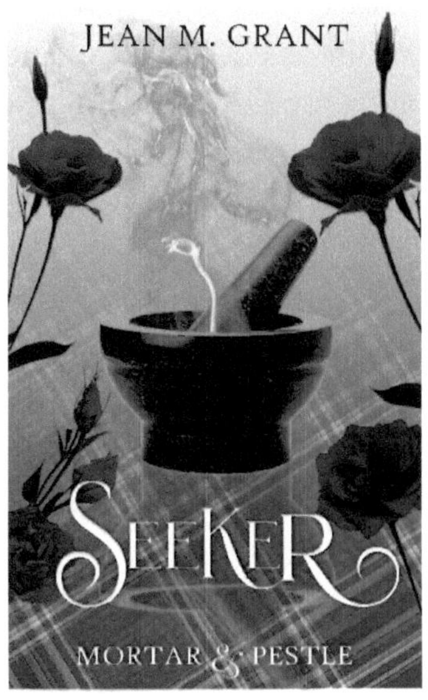

Book 2: Seeker by Jean M. Grant

Journey from the land of selkies and Norse longships across the Nord Sea to fourteenth-century Scotland. Home to craggy mountains, stalwart castles, and expansive moorland, both superstition and strength of the blade guide the Highland clans. Will the magic of the Mortar & Pestle unite the tenuous alliance among the Montgomeries and MacDougalls, or cleave it, bringing them to war?

Nock, draw, release. Her bow is always ready, and if her arrow hits its mark, she will secure her destined soulmate.

Aileana Montgomerie's bloodline holds valuable gifts of foresight and healing, but with each honor comes a curse. Even though she is descended from the mystical isles' folk, she lacks the ability of the Scottish Ancients and wonders if she belongs in a magical family. Aileana just wants a purpose. What good is her bow and arrow if she is denied the right to fight for her clan?

Brodie MacDougall is ordained to be the next war chieftain of his clan. The title is a privilege as long as his brother, the future laird, doesn't expect him to lift a sword and charge into battle. Chronic pain and nervous vapors force him to spend his days alone. Can his strategic skills keep him one step ahead of his conspiring brother?

Through a magical Mortar & Pestle, Brodie finds his heart's desire. But there's a catch. The seat on his brother's council is no longer dependent upon his health…but on Aileana's strength. With rumblings of unrest among their clans, will their love foster an alliance or be a step toward war?

More Stories from The Mortar and Pestle Series:

Book 3: Quartermaster by Marilyn Barr

Catalina

He violated me. Don Rodrigo took my family's business, home, and titles, but he will never own me. I'm on the run. He's threatened to expose my secret. My last hope is to intercept the ship carrying my dowry before our match is permanent. Trusting pirates to give me a fair share is foolish but not as much as staying on the same island as my attacker…

Chub

The letter from our arch-nemesis was written in feminine calligraphy but our nutmeg Captain Teeth didn't notice. Blimey that because the author of the letter is my lady love. I'd bet my last doubloon. If only she didn't shrink away from my touch… Killing every scoundrel who dared to hurt her isn't helping…but it cools the rage I hold inside.

Can Chub teach Catalina to assemble her shattered fragments into the strong woman she wants to be or is she too broken to believe in herself? Will she accept a pirate's promise of true love or was the Mortar & Pestle's message too late for lonely Chub to claim his lady love?

Book 4: Sea Hunter by D.V. Stone

On the turbulent high seas, an archeologist must protect a historic shipwreck from treasure hunters—not fall for one.

Zahra Corbyn

As the professor of antiquities, nothing snaps my cap more than treasure hunters and looters. They smash and grab and then are gone with the wind. And there are two after Sea Wraith. But fate is a funny thing. Thanks to an ancient Mortar & Pestle, not only am I in cahoots with one of them but he's also fired up my heart, turning me into a khaki-wacky.

Captain Jack Alexander

I've been told women on a ship are unlucky, but this dame has the two pieces of the map I need to finally claim Sea Wraith. Now, I find myself in a lousy deal that makes me one-third partner with her and a known scalawag. It's either that or bupkis. After all these years of chasing down my dream of finding the shipwreck, my obsession is cooling off and heating up toward a bird who's way above my pay grade.
Can the two unlikely allies work together while safeguarding their hearts against the power of the Mortar & Pestle?

If you like Lara Croft and Indiana Jones, you'll love Zahra Corbyn and Jack Alexander.

Book 5: Revamped by Shirley Goldberg

Vampire Dante Allegretti hates his sucky life. Born into a family of energy siphoners, he's desperate to reinvent himself as a fun-loving normal guy rather than a crowdsourcing parasite. To stop the draining urges, Dante resorts to grinding alternative meds in an ancient Mortar & Pestle, not knowing it contains magical properties.

Enter wisecracking thirty-year-old Sophie Arley, who lives with her clingy parents. Working three jobs and craving independence, she's come back strong after a breakdown crashed her cozy world. So when the weird, hot guy she just met-cute asks Sophie to the movies, she agrees.

Sophie won't spoil their magical connection by mentioning her heartbreak. And Dante dreads telling Sophie about his dark side. Will the power from the Mortar & Pestle guide them to their happily ever after despite the secrets and lies?

Book 6: Trickster by Darlene Fredette

Working for a top modeling agency is Jade Parsons's dream job until her boss suffers a heart attack, and his son temporarily fills his position. Eric's push-pull approach fuels her frustration. While anticipating the troublemaker's imminent departure, Jade's destiny is revealed through a magical mortar and pestle, leaving her heart tormented by whispers of a different fate.

World-renowned photographer Eric Martini returns home to restore his relationship with his estranged father, but wounds from the past haunt him. Enchanted by his father's feisty assistant, he masks his heart and refuses to give in to desire. Convinced his destined future is already written in the stars—and doesn't include Jade, Eric's only choice is to walk away.

Book 7: Artist by Ginny Frost

Lexi Pintari is stuck in a dead-end cubicle job that is slowly killing her. She tucked away her passion for art when the love of her life ghosted her after college. Witnessing her lack of motivation, Lexi's best friend drags her to an art retreat for much-needed reflection and inspiration. Though knowing her ex-boyfriend is an artist-in-residence there, Lexi agrees to go. Unfortunately, her metal-goth style and enthusiasm for graphic comics clash with the pastel-scarf-wearing, tea-sipping participants, making her ex the least of her problems.

Cole MacDougall is blocked. His rise to the top of the modern art scene is crushed by a missing muse. He is desperate to paint again, but the canvas remains blank. Due to the shortage of patronage revenue, he is forced to put up with the groupie-students. Until he sees a woman standing out like a sore thumb in ripped jeans and a leather jacket. Lexi. Hope blooms that he can renew his passion through her.

For two weeks, Lexi and Cole work together, discovering what they've lost professionally and personally. Will a magical mortar and pestle show them how to connect the broken lines and seal their destiny?

Sneak Peak of A Breath of Sunlight

Prologue

Today was the day the king of the fae was to choose his bride.

Sunshine rained down from pink-lined clouds like drops of gold. It glistened and sparkled and beamed, its energy strong on the summer solstice in the Sun Kingdom of Heulwen. Laughter rang out in the castle courtyard as men and women alike from all over the kingdom gathered for the upcoming festivities. Many stood near the large, circular fountain while others conversed on a well-manicured lawn. Golden ribbons stretched from pillar to pillar while flowers of garlands, wreaths, and bouquets littered the large area.

Calle Everdon wrung his hands, pacing back and forth beside the window. Sunshine filtered through the glass pane, and while he usually considered it a welcoming companion, it glanced right off his skin as if sensing his anxious energy.

He gazed out at the women below as they entered the castle. Many wore crowns of flowers. Their emotions lay transparent on their faces. Lips twisted with anxiety. Eyebrows furrowed with both worry and determination. Eyes brightened with hope.

Calle ran an anxious hand over the scratchy stubble on his face. All the unmarried women were to attend the celebration.

All of them.

On cue, his sweetheart, Nyana, slipped through the door, a comb placed in a simple blonde bun. Her light blue dress was plain and unadorned—a similar style to a servant's—unlike her usual clothing.

She rushed into his arms, and he clung tightly to her as if she might be yanked out of his life at any moment.

At the thought, he clung tighter.

"Calle," she murmured as she pushed him away to hold him at arm's length. He reluctantly obliged. Her long, gentle fingers smoothed each eyebrow, his high cheekbones, and finally lovingly traced the long points of his fae ears. "Don't fret over this. Everything will turn out fine."

"How do you know?" He searched her blue eyes for a sliver of truth within their depths. "How do you know my brother won't choose you?"

"Because I have taken every precaution possible to avoid his notice. I look plain, don't I?"

She smiled brightly, her aura radiant as she turned in a full circle. A lump formed in his dry throat. "No," he rasped. "You could never look plain."

He grabbed her hand and pulled her closer until their foreheads touched. An ache of longing solidified in his gut. "I beg you, Nyana. Run away with me. Leave all this behind."

The tension in the air thickened, slicing through the excited laughter coming from outside. Unease churned within him, and only increased tenfold at her answer. "You know we cannot run. You are a prince, Calle. You have duties to your people. Running today of all days would mean treason on both our heads."

"But I can't lose you."

"And you won't," she whispered, cradling his face. "I won't stand out amongst hundreds of other women. He won't single me out. He won't pick me."

"*I* would pick you." He squeezed her shoulders and gazed at her with a serious expression. "You know he takes everything I want."

"But he doesn't know about us, and he won't until after he has chosen his bride."

An easier breath filled his lungs, and he let it out slowly. She was right. He was paranoid, and rightly so. He and Nyana had only dared to court in secret—without his brother's knowledge. He couldn't bear to lose her. It would break him.

Her soothing touch moved to his neck-length red-brown hair. Each stroke of her fingers cooled the burning anxiety rising within him.

"I wish I could heal you in here," she said, placing her hand over his heart after a few moments of comfortable silence. "But I am not capable of magic like you."

Not all Sun Fae were capable of magic, like Nyana and Calle's older brother, Liam. Liam overcompensated for his lack of talent with his cruelty and unending jealousy. They were always at odds with one another.

Calle grimaced and rubbed the scar over his gold-tattooed wrist where Liam had sliced him to the bone during a fit of anger. Heulwen's skilled healers had saved his hand, but only just. Perhaps "at odds" was too tame a term for their relationship.

"Is your hand bothering you today?" she asked, a frown on her pretty face.

He shook his head, his eyebrows furrowing at the twelve-pointed Heulwen scar tattoo. It gleamed beneath the sunlight like golden lava. "Just trapped in the past. Promise me, Nyana," he glanced nervously toward the door as if someone in the hallway might overhear their hushed conversation, "stay out of Liam's view. He'll find a way to take you. I know he will."

"I promise." She pressed a lingering kiss to his lips before giving him yet another radiant smile. "And after this is all over, we can court in the open."

Golden streams of magic flowed out of his fingertips like a gentle river. He coaxed the magic until it formed the shape of a flower. He tucked the flower into her hair, knowing she'd take it out before anyone else noticed. "I'm looking forward to the day."

Their hands slid out of each other's in farewell. His gaze lingered on her long after she left. The heat slowly left the room as if a cloud blocked out her warm presence. A chill shook him to the bones—one consisting of relentless dread. Deep in his gut, his magic churned with trepidation. Something didn't feel right.

Taking a deep breath calmed his overbearing nerves. He straightened his clothing and exited the small drawing room in the east wing of the castle. Servants bustled past him with food piled high on golden platters for the summer solstice celebrations. The scents of cheese, wild boar, and spiced wine didn't entice him, but rather drew anxiety further out of his core.

He greeted many people by name on his way, until his friend, Joel, fell into step beside him. His brown hair fell across his forehead, his green eyes seeing far more than one expected. He possessed sun magic, but his came in the form of music. He could charm any animal into submission or strike peace in a room with only a few notes. An artist at heart with his head forever in the clouds.

"I've figured it out," Joel said without preamble as he flipped through a book filled with notes in his nearly indecipherable handwriting. "Liam has a very small chance of picking Nyana to become—"

"Shh!" Calle hissed as he pushed his friend into the shadows, only to suck in a pained breath when the action sent a jolt of agony through his wrist. He cradled his hand to his chest as he glanced each way down the hallway, but no one appeared to have heard the comment. "You know you can't say her name. Not yet."

Joel scrunched his eyebrows together, his fingers resting on the flute tied to his belt as if ready to draw it and use it as a weapon. "One song, and I think I can hide her from his view."

With a sigh, Calle shook his head. His entire body was both weary to the bone and fully alert. "Liam has his own disenchanters. It will only draw more notice."

His wrist still throbbed as they continued down the hallway, following hundreds of others into a vast courtyard. The music grew louder with each step, as did the number of guards. Fae guards wore the kingdom's colors—red and gold—on a generic uniform. However, surrounding Liam at the top of the steps…

The royal palace guards stood alert, each harpy wearing gold armor and a red cape over one shoulder with the Heulwen emblem on their breast. Their wings were tucked neatly behind their backs, but Calle had seen those wings unfurl faster than one could blink. Harpies were dangerous, but he counted himself lucky they served the royal family. On the day of a harpy's birth, they were sworn into a blood oath to protect the royal family of the Sun Kingdom to their very last breath.

Each of the harpies—both men and women—bowed to him as he approached and created a path for him to join Liam's side. Joel found a place on the other side of the courtyard near the musicians.

Calle straightened his crown and smoothed his clothing as he looked over the crowd. Laughter and radiant, excited smiles had joined the music. He marveled at how many women were in attendance, each competing to stand out from the crowd. Some wore their hair down around their shoulders. Others wore crowns of flowers or sunlight. But none were as beautiful as the woman who held his heart.

Releasing a deep breath of relief, his shoulders relaxed. There were far too many choices for Liam to notice Nyana.

He quickly spotted her small frame in a group of five other women. Her gentle features were pulled into an anxious strain, her mouth pinched. They made eye contact across the courtyard but glanced away just as fast.

"You seem nervous, Calle," Liam chuckled beside him, and he jumped at the sudden, unwelcome intrusion. It took all his self-control not to glance back in Nyana's direction.

"I'm simply curious about which one of these lovely women you will choose for your wife," he replied in a steady voice. His mouth twitched as he feigned amusement. "I can't help but wonder who will be left for me."

Liam clapped him on the back a bit harder than a friendly pat. "You will get your turn when you turn twenty-one next year. But the question is…will you choose beauty or an advantageous match?"

The vein in his neck pulsed with every pounding heartbeat even as he gave a nonchalant shrug. The Everdon royal family had chosen their spouses this way for many generations, and even though their parents had both passed, he and Liam continued the tradition. In the past, women already a part of the court had been chosen, but every once in a while, a beauty from an outlying village would turn an eye.

"I suppose I will find out when the time comes."

Relax, he ordered his body. It refused to cooperate.

He eyed the sword, which had been directed at him more than once, tied to Liam's belt. At one time, he'd wielded a greatsword himself, but since the "accident", magic was his only weapon.

It churned within him, begging to be released.

He reined it in.

"I'll get straight to the point," Liam said as he turned slowly, a dark glint in his cobalt-green eyes. "Today is an important day. If you so much as step out of line once, I will show no mercy."

A harpy guard beside him, Avonia, shifted her unique white wings with a golden shimmer, but otherwise kept her eyes forward and a hand on her sword. She and her husband, Typheal, were good friends of his. They'd had a daughter once named Scarlett, but she had been abducted on her first birthday fourteen years ago. He remembered the panic and absolute terror of the event. Her parents still grieved the loss to this day.

Calle flexed his injured hand as he nodded half-heartedly. He would die before he let Liam anywhere near Nyana. He hoped it wouldn't escalate to blows between him and his brother.

As if appeased, Liam's smile returned as he scanned the crowd. His gaze stopped on…

No…

But the look had been so fleeting, and it could have been anyone in Nyana's group.

Uneasiness knocked the breath out of him. He sucked in a gulp of air, wishing to hold onto something to steady himself.

Liam's grin grew wide as he spotted someone in the crowd. He jogged down the stone steps to greet them, leaving him with half the harpy warriors while the other half followed. Avonia and Typheal moved to stand on either side of him. Their presence helped calm the storm raging within him.

"We won't let him lay a finger on you," Avonia murmured, her eyes hard. Typheal nodded in agreement.

"You must." His throat bobbed up and down as he swallowed. Finally, he tore his gaze away from his brother's back to look at the two people who had been like family for as long as he remembered. "I know something bad is going to happen. I can feel it in my gut. I couldn't live with myself if something happened to you two."

Typheal answered this time, the natural golden strands in his brown hair glimmering beneath the afternoon rays. "We may be blood bound to both you and the king, but we are loyal to you. Whatever happens…we are with you."

He swallowed again, grateful for their undying loyalty.

He cast another glance in Nyana's direction. She turned as if feeling his gaze on her and placed her hand against her heart. *I love you*, the gesture said. He raised a hand to do the same, but someone clamped their fingers around his wrist.

Pain shot up his arm and through his hand, enough to nearly buckle his knees. He sucked in a breath and barely held in a cry.

"Come," Liam said as he tugged him down the steps. "There are several people I want to introduce you to."

Pain pulsed through Calle's wrist with each beat of his heart. The day passed agonizingly slowly as young ladies captured every moment of Liam's attention. Music and laughter made a mockery of the rainclouds in his soul. On more than one occasion, he nearly grabbed Nyana's hand and pulled her away from the festivities to the freedom that awaited outside the kingdom. But she was right. They would be hunted. Running was no way to live.

Afternoon transitioned to dusk. Torches burst to life in the courtyard, illuminating everyone's animated expressions. Shallow breaths entered Calle's lungs as he stood at the top of the steps, several feet behind his brother.

Liam held out his arms, and the entire courtyard quieted to hear his words. "My loyal subjects! I am pleased to have met many new faces today, and rekindled relationships with some old as we celebrate the summer solstice. As is tradition on one's twenty-first birthday, I am to choose a bride tonight. If you are not picked, do not be discouraged. You might have a chance with Prince Calle next year."

The crowd rumbled with excited chatter, even as Liam cast Calle a mocking grin as if he were leftovers and not the main course.

He clenched his right fist as hard as he could while his left remained limp at his side. He could not do much with his non-dominant hand other than hold light objects.

"Without further ado…" Liam strode down the steps in Nyana's direction. Dread pounded into him like a relentless rainstorm, at least until his brother glanced over his shoulder and cast him a wicked grin. His blood flooded with a river of ice.

Liam knew.

He'd always known.

Calle dashed down the steps with panic nipping at his heels. He shoved his brother aside right as he reached for Nyana's hand and stood protectively in front of her with outstretched arms.

The courtyard fell into a shocked hush as he stared back into Liam's furious eyes.

"Touch her," Calle hissed, not caring who heard him speak, "and I will kill you."

It was not an empty threat.

Nyana's gentle fingers gripped the back of his shirt, and although he didn't turn to see her expression, he felt fear emanating from her. He could only imagine what awful things Liam would do to her if they married. He'd beaten a couple women he'd courted, one of them nearly to the brink of death. Nyana's sweet, tender spirit couldn't survive a husband like Liam. Likely everyone in the kingdom knew— or at least suspected—Liam was capable of abuse and cruelty. But he was the king. Who could stop him?

"Step aside," Liam growled.

"Never."

"I warned you if you stepped out of line, I would show no mercy. Come here, little chit."

"No," she answered in a quivering tone.

When Liam began to reach out again, Calle hit his hand aside. Foreboding silence echoed around them as everyone watched. Guards stood on the tips of their toes as if ready to jump in at a moment's notice.

"You can have anyone you want—just not her," he begged.

Nyana's fingers trembled against his back when anger smoldered hotter in Liam's eyes. Color climbed his brother's neck, wounded pride rising with it. Calle's own hands shook. Whenever he'd hurt Liam's pride in the past, the next few minutes usually ended in bloodshed.

"Please," he begged again. He would have collapsed to his knees and kissed his brother's feet if it would have made a difference, but he didn't dare leave Nyana unprotected.

Liam ground his teeth together, his fingers now resting on the sword on his belt. "Step. Aside. Your king has spoken."

Instead of succumbing to Liam's unspoken threat, Nyana wrapped her arms around Calle's waist from behind, making her choice. He attempted to swallow his fear, but it remained lodged in his throat. They should have escaped the city when they'd still had the chance. Now he'd have to fight, and he wasn't sure he could win.

He eyed Liam's sword, the harpies standing at his back, and the hundreds of spectators standing between him and the nearest exit.

Before he had another second to evaluate his surroundings, Liam drew his sword with frightening speed and swung it toward him. A surge of magic rippled through him, and he raised his arms in time to block the attack with a sturdy rod created from ribbons of magic. A *clang* echoed through the courtyard. His hand protested at the effort to keep his brother's weapon at bay. Liam pressed harder, and his fingers slipped. He slammed his magic into Liam's chest. His brother flew several feet before he smashed into the fountain.

Water splashed around him, the cherub's bow breaking in half against the blow.

"Go!" he cried as he pushed Nyana into the chaotic crowd. People screamed as they fled the scene. "Don't look back. You know where to meet me."

"Calle," she sobbed, her blue eyes wide. "I can't leave you."

He pulled her against him and crushed her lips with his own. "Go," he said again in a husky whisper. "I'll be right behind you."

He turned just in time to block the next attack from his enraged brother. Liam's eyes were bloodshot, sticky ribbons of blood dripping from his hairline. Liam smashed his sword against his magic rod once, twice, three times, until his weapon shattered into golden dust. He rolled out of the way of the next swing, but he wasn't fast enough to avoid the tip of the sword slicing his left shoulder.

A cry of pain escaped him. His arm refused to lift when Liam swiped at him again. He ducked the attack and kicked him in the knee, producing a loud *crack*. His brother's howl stirred the harpies loyal to Liam into action. Three harpies tackled Calle to the ground. Someone held an arm against his throat, choking the air from him. Black dots fizzled into the edges of his vision as he clawed and kicked and punched. Magic heated his hand, and the moment he touched it against the arm on his throat, the harpy hissed and flinched away. He gasped in a breath of air, only for his windpipe to get blocked by another arm.

Just when his vision threatened to fade completely, the weight on top of him disappeared.

He gasped in breath after breath as he sat up in a daze. Avonia and Typheal were fighting to protect him.

Sunlight fueled him as he charged forward and locked himself in battle once again with Liam—rod against sword. He struggled to keep up with Liam's strength when one arm still hung uselessly at his side, even as his brother limped and favored one leg. But he didn't need to win. He only needed to distract him long enough for Nyana to escape.

Calle dodged Liam's lunge and managed to disarm him with a lucky hit to his hand. Calle tackled his brother to the ground, and they traded blows with fists. Magic stirred within him as he punched him in the jaw. Heat blasted out from his fist and seared one side of Liam's face. Liam screamed and clutched the burn that stretched from his forehead to his jaw.

Not daring to stay a single moment longer, he pushed up from the ground and sprinted toward an exit. But in a blindingly fast movement, a harpy dropped down in front of him and kicked him in the chest.

The air *whooshed* from his lungs as he stumbled backward, and he couldn't right himself before he was pinned to the ground again, two sets of brown wings blocking his view of the sky.

One of the harpies turned him around and smashed his face into the ground, arms pinned on either side of him.

But then his entire world froze as if encased in a block of ice. He ceased struggling, his eyes wide. Liam's scarred face contorted with anger as he held a fistful of blonde hair in one hand, and his sword in the other. The weapon protruded from Nyana's creamy skin. Her face twisted with pain as blood soaked the front of her gown.

Calle screamed her name and struggled against his captors with every ounce of strength and magic he possessed. But just as he escaped, another couple of harpies pinned him again.

Tears streamed down his face as he watched Nyana slump to the ground. Her chin trembled. Her fingers shook. And then her body became still as the life left her eyes.

"No," he sobbed. "No!"

Again, he screamed her name, but she didn't respond. He attempted to free himself from the weight on top of him to get to her, but he only cried out when Liam stepped on his left wrist and ground his boot until only a fiery trail of agony remained.

"You have defied me for the last time," Liam spat, his words stilted by the burn tugging on his lip. "I will make sure you never again see the light of day."

"Go to h—"

Something heavy smashed against the back of his head, and darkness quickly shrouded his vision. The last thing he was aware of was heat searing into his forearm before his consciousness became as black as the midnight sky.

ABOUT THE AUTHOR

Sydney Winward is an award-winning fantasy and paranormal romance author who dabbles in the occasional historical fiction. She loves building complex worlds filled with magic, strong characters, and emotional stories that can make you laugh and cry.

Sydney is the author of the bestselling Bloodborn Series, and when she's not writing, she's reading, thinking about stories, or going on adventures with her children. She lives in Utah with her husband and three amazing kids.

www.sydneywinward.com